To my family and friends who support and encourage me.

Experience is the hardest teacher.

It gives you the test first and the lesson afterwards.

OSCAR WILDE

ISBN-978-1-7391799-8-4

ISBN-978-1-7391799-9-1

Cover design by: Art Painter
Library of Congress Control Number: 2018675309
Printed in the United States of America

CONTENTS

PREFACE

I have observed a man like David MacDonald, a sensitive and caring man, attractive in character and body.

Talented, yet totally lacking in confidence, with so much to give in exchange for so little.

A man that women adore as a friend and confidant but who is forever alone, always the bachelor.

It's a strange and interesting combination and one that led me to write the Widow's Friend

WIDOW' S FRIEND

CHAPTER 1

My name is David McDonald, I was born in Edinburgh on December 24th1950. I suppose you could say that I had a charmed childhood, the only offspring of Harriet and James McDonald, no siblings to compete with for attention, everything I ever needed provided.

I have always considered myself a Scotsman although I have never actually lived there. My family were decidedly middle class, my father a Captain in the Scots Guards, mother a full-time homemaker. By the time I reached five years old, mum and I had been parked in a 1930s semi-detached in Caterham, Surrey, near to the barracks where dad's division had been stationed for three years.

Our house was a three bed semi in a quiet suburban road, built after the Second World War to accommodate the growing ranks of London commuters. With a direct line to Charing Cross it was a popular place to purchase a modest home away from the dirty chaos of London. Good schools and a close proximity to the countryside and in particular the South Downs made for the popularity of the ever expanding green belt. A combination of taste and Scottish meanness had saved our red bricks from the almost compulsory pebble-dashing that was so popular at the time. The interior of the semi was a muted brown and beige, with mostly strong wooden furniture, made to last. The only exception was the modern Formica kitchen in a sunny yellow that my mum loved, and where she spent most of her time. My father found the garish colours of the early sixties quite offensive and certainly not to his taste.

When my dad's regiment packed up and moved on, my father dutifully followed from barracks to barracks, country to country, whilst my mother and I remained in Caterham.

Dad had decided that it was not for us to be dragged around; I needed stability, not the traveller lifestyle of the regiment. It meant that I saw very little of my father over the next few years. When he did come home he seemed terrifyingly strict. A terrible gloom settled over our lives, my relaxed and spoilt existence totally changed during those nightmare visits. Fortunately for me, as time went by his appearances became less frequent. Alone with my mother, I was allowed to do all the things I enjoyed most.

My mother encouraged me to do the things that she loved. I learnt to play the piano to a good standard but it was ballroom dancing that became our passion. Three times a week after school, mum picked me up in our new Morris Minor and whisked me off to the practice sessions with our local group. I became a very good dancer and by the time I was fifteen I had joined the famous Frank and Peggy Spencer Dancing School in Penge, Southeast London, where they taught absolute beginners to top professionals. My mother was ecstatic and never complained about the long drives to and from home in the evenings.

I was encouraged to enter competitions, which I began to win, and danced in the Frank and Peggy Spencer formation dancing team appearing on Come Dancing, a hugely popular TV show of the time. Of course I didn't dare share any of that with my school mates, I doubt that I would have had an easy time, not in those days. I would definitely have been called a sissy. I continued dancing until I eventually went to the University of Kent where I studied for a degree in English Literature.

Strangely, my father had never objected to my dancing, he had some old fashioned notion that a gentleman should know how to foxtrot or waltz. Apparently, he was skilled in the ballroom himself, although I never witnessed any of that talent myself. It didn't seem possible that such a serious and sedentary man would have ever enjoyed such sensuous abandonment.

As small silver gilt cups started to arrive in the glass cabinet in our front room, I observed him once or twice pick up a new addition and study it at length.

By the time I went to the University of Kent in 1968 my father had retired from the army, he'd eventually reached the dizzy heights of major and luckily had a decent pension. At least my mother wasn't alone at home after I left and that was a consolation to me, as I worried about her. I knew my dad couldn't replace the joy we had shared all those years through the dancing, but at least he was there to keep her busy with his ever increasing ailments and demands.

I didn't keep up my dancing at University, it wasn't cool, and cool was everything in 1968. I wasn't that popular and found it hard to make friends, but unlike so many of my contemporaries, I kept my head down and studied. The results reflected my hard work and only enhanced my reputation for being boring, consequently I didn't get a girlfriend until my final year. Rachel was a fellow English student, I had noticed her looking at me a few times but honestly she was quite frightening. An ardent feminist with a brilliant debating record, she had an answer to nearly everything, and I was completely out of my depth. I think she felt sorry for me, although I wasn't ugly. I had a delicate look, like I was slowly dying. Tall, with regular features, really nothing wrong but nothing notable, not the athletic body that I admired on some of the other male students. I had tried to build up a bit but found I lacked the enthusiasm for any of the more macho sports like football or rugby, although I was handy on the cricket team during the summer months.

The thick shock of black curly hair that corkscrewed out of Rachel's head extended to all parts of her body, she was by far the hairiest girl I have ever met. Of course she shaved nothing, it wasn't necessary to conform to the fifty's ideal of the all American girl anymore. She was liberated from that crap, proudly denigrating her Jewish family, stating that it wasn't logical to follow any religion. She was an atheist, the only way to be for modern thinkers like me and her.

I didn't know what I thought. I suppose I was Church of Scotland like my mum and dad, I'd never given it much thought. But for all our thoroughly modern outlook, it took until after the last exam and the end of our studies before we finally consummated our friendship into an actual, real sexual experience.

Everybody was celebrating. Rachel and I met with a crowd at the student's union bar and we all got absolutely hammered on cheap Mateus Rose wine and pints of watery beer. The whole evening was like a surreal dream, I was aware but not really in control of my faculties or my limbs. I remember being sick at least once, walking back to the student accommodation, singing and generally being in an unusually rowdy state. How I ended up waking up in Rachel's bed eludes me to this day, but she assured me that neither of us were still virgins. Great, it was a disgrace to get to twenty-one and still be a virgin, but I would like to have been present for the momentous act! However, I was present for the follow up in the morning, much to my consternation. I had never even seen my mother naked, and I'm sure that she wouldn't have had the enormous black bush of pubic hair that was nestled between Rachel's legs. I was shocked, I wasn't sure I would be able to find the place to put my shrivelled penis. I valiantly persisted and thanked God that neither of us were experienced enough to expect anything better than the feeble effort of pushing and grunting that ensued.

The next day, the end of the University year, we were getting ready to leave for home. My mother came to pick me up as I had acquired quite a few books and other possessions during my three year stint at Kent. I was mortified as we packed the car to see Rachel running across the green waving at me. I didn't want my mother to meet my newfound love, and Rachel made it worse by throwing herself at me and crying about how much she would miss me, to keep in touch and that we should meet in London during the holidays.

"Who is that?" My mum looked slightly nonplussed, as she whispered behind a discreet hand. There had been no mention of any girlfriends in any of my letters or during my holidays home.

"Mum, this is Rachel, my friend," I explained, trying to unwrap her arms from around my neck.

"So nice to meet you Mrs McDonald." All the Jewish girl politeness back and the raging militant gone. "I do hope to be able to visit you during the holidays, David and I have become quite close." She smiled secretly up at me and I felt my face burning with embarrassment.

"Of course, any friend of David is always welcome." My mother gracious in her British, middle-class way.

Finally, we managed to get all my things packed away into our little car with Rachel's help, and I waved goodbye as she dabbed a tissue to her weeping eyes and running nose.

"Well," was all my mother added, sensing my deep desire to put the whole scene behind me.

After a suitable break, she casually mentioned that dad had spoken to an old army colleague and that he had managed to get me an interview for a junior job in the foreign office. I didn't care as long as she didn't ask me any awkward questions about Rachel.

CHAPTER 2

We drove down our quiet tree lined road of semi-detached residences and pulled up on the steep drive outside the house. I noticed our next door neighbour twitch her curtain. Of course they were all expecting me, news that I was on my way home was about as much excitement as you could expect in a street that housed mainly retired gentle folk. My dad came to the door, his appearance shockingly changed since my last visit at Christmas time. He leaned heavily on his walking stick and looked at least ten years older.

"I can't help. Sorry son," he called from the doorstep.

"It's okay dad, I can manage. Don't mum," I called out gesturing to all the luggage as she went to help. "You go and put the tea on. I can do this in no time."

When did my parents suddenly get so old? How had I not noticed before?

By the time I'd finished dragging my things up the narrow staircase to my old bedroom and locked the car door, mum and dad were sitting patiently with the best teapot, cups and saucers and some McVities chocolate biscuits on a matching plate, all carefully arranged on the kitchen table. I felt like a guest, it was odd. We never used the 'best' set of crockery normally. We sat quietly, sipping our tea and crunching the biscuits.

"I suppose mum told you on the drive here, I managed to get old Smythe to give you a recommendation to his office. It's a good start, you can go up the ladder from there." My dad still had the faint remnants of his Scottish accent.

"Yes, mum told me, thank you dad. I appreciate your help."

"Well, it's the least I could do, we are all very proud of you son." No McDonald had ever been to University before, after all it was only for academics and wasn't necessary to get a regular job in 1971.

I didn't know if I wanted to work in an office, but dad was right, you had to start somewhere and I would certainly need to get a job as soon as possible. There was no question of adult children being supported by parents, I had already learned hard enough financial lessons just to get through three years at University, although I'd done a few casual jobs during the holidays. I would go for the interview the next week and see how I got on. At least I would pass the security checks, there would be no thought that I was a left wing activist or any such thing, especially when my dad was a retired army major. I was relieved now that I hadn't let Rachel suck me into joining the communist party when she had joined a few months back.

The interview day arrived and I dutifully put on a grey suit and headed up to town on the 8.45 train for my 10.00 am appointment. I was met by Simon Smythe the epitome of an ex regimental man. Large moustache and expanded middle, a rather ruddy complexion from too much rich food and alcohol. He patted me on the back and asked after my father 'Jamie.'

"He's well sir," I responded politely even though that wasn't strictly true. My dad wouldn't have been happy for me to reveal his failing health.

The interview was only an hour, the panel asked me questions about my time at the University of Kent. When asked about hobbies, I revealed my previous commitment to ballroom dancing which although lapsed, was something I really wanted to go back to once I had settled my unemployment status. Mrs Grey, one of the panel, was suitably impressed that I had been one of the Frank and Peggy Spencer formation team and said she was a fan of Come Dancing. The whole interview seemed reasonable and as I left, Smythe was waiting to take me to lunch at his club.

We took a taxi to the RAC Club in Pall Mall, even though it would have been a pleasant 10 minute walk for me. I guessed by his girth that Smythe didn't do too much walking. I had never been to such an opulent place, the beautiful building next to St James Palace was famed for its dining room and you could easily see why. The service was impeccable, black suited waiters hovered to attend to your every need. Smythe ordered his usual bottle of claret which was sublime and left me slightly giddy. The filet mignon melted in your mouth and the dessert trolly was a veritable feast for the eyes. Smythe had a dessert and a cheese selection with a large vintage port that I had to decline. I couldn't imagine how this man would be able to return to his office and do any work during the afternoon.

I felt quite sick on the homeward train journey to Caterham. Smythe had insisted on taking me to Charing Cross in a taxi, and I honestly would have preferred to walk some of my excellent but extremely rich lunch off. Both my parents were anxious to hear about my experience, and all I could say is that it had all gone well as far as I could tell. I elaborated more on my lunch with Smythe and hoped that if I got the job I wouldn't be expected to lunch like that too often. My dad seemed pleased, which counted for much more.

Every day it bothered me that my father seemed to be getting up later and doing less. I just naturally filled in and accompanied my mother to appointments and helped her with shopping and practical things around the home.

I was beginning to become anxious after two weeks of hearing nothing, when the letter arrived offering me the job as clerk to the Under Secretary at the Foreign Office. The starting salary was £2,080pa which was far more that I had expected from my first job. I immediately sat down and replied with a letter of acceptance. I told mother that I would be able to give her £5 per week for my keep and she was over the moon.

"That's very generous of you David, thank you."

My mother had only ever had housekeeping money to control, all the bills and banking were dealt with by my father. She had no idea what the electricity or the gas cost, if there was a mortgage on the house or indeed if my father had gambled away all their savings. He put her shopping money on the table every Friday and she used it to feed us and make sure the house looked nice. Any major expenditure had to be approved by my father, and he would organise payment. There was never any real discussion, that's the way things were and nobody even considered rocking the boat, least of all my gentle mother. The only area that she had any kind of autonomy over was the car. Strangely enough, my father had bought her the car when he was still in the army and spending months away. It was her pride and joy and she had learned to drive quickly and easily, it was her route to any kind of freedom and had been essential for me to attend my dancing classes.

My father could drive, he had learnt in the army, but he didn't since becoming ill, it tired him too much. Mum decided it was time for me to learn and she booked and paid for my first ten lessons with the British School of Motoring. The instructor would pick me up every Saturday morning and we would drive in a complicated pattern around Caterham, do a three point turn in the same cul de sac and use the same road to practice the reversing around a corner routine. Luckily, I had inherited my mother's skill for driving and I easily passed my test first time and the whole family celebrated with a special tea. My mum baked a cake that nearly resembled a car, not quite, but it was still delicious.

***

Then in September my father suddenly died. We were shocked, for although we had both witnessed his steady decline, when the time finally came it was like a huge hole had opened up in the middle of the house and he was just swallowed up.

I heard my mother's scream; it was a Saturday morning and I was sleeping in. I jumped out of bed and rushed to the alarming sound.

My father looked asleep, my mother was standing crying, her hand shaking but still holding the cup and saucer containing the tea she had come to give him. I gently took the tea from her and placed it on the bedside table, then I steered her away and downstairs. There was nothing to achieve by her standing there traumatised. I sat her at the kitchen table and found a box of tissues, then I made us a cup of tea and stood near her. She clung to me sobbing. I suppose that I must have been distressed but I didn't really register that this was real. It was my mother's anguish that was most upsetting.

After a few minutes, I felt that I needed to do something.

"Mum, you just stay here, I'll call Dr Burke. He will know what we have to do now."

She just nodded; it was heart-breaking. I never really considered if my parents loved each other, I just thought that they must do, but theirs had been such a subdued and formal marriage. I had never witnessed any passion, good or bad. No drama, no arguments, no tender moments or anything else. I kind of thought all parents were like that. I suppose you could say that is what had stunted my own emotional development, made me grey and boring way before my time.

Dr Burke arrived, and I followed him upstairs. It was the first time I had really looked at a dead body. My father was strangely peaceful, lying still in his pyjamas; he looked normal, just asleep. I'm not sure what I expected, but not that. The doctor pronounced him dead after a short examination and covered his face with the sheet, then we went back to my mother who was still sitting numbly at the kitchen table, nursing the empty cup in her shaking hand. I took it from her and offered the doctor a tea as I refreshed her cup from the teapot.

"Do you have any family you can call to comfort your mother?" Dr Burke enquired.

"Nobody that I know. My mother has a sister in Scotland somewhere, I don't think they are close, I've never met them." It stuck me how odd it was that we had no close family or friends, no female group who could rally around my mum to help her through her grief. Only me.

The doctor used the phone to call the local undertaker. He would come and remove the body although it wouldn't be till later in the day. I was very grateful to the doctor for his advice and help, and that my dad would not have to spend the weekend dead in his bed upstairs. That just seemed all wrong and I didn't think mum would be able to cope with him lying there.

True to his word, Chappell and Son turned up during the afternoon and with a sombre formality reassured us that they would handle everything from there on. We would have to visit their office in the High Street on Monday morning to discuss funeral arrangements. They discreetly left a brochure on our hall table and shook my hand before transporting dad away. It would be the last time either of us saw him; such a final goodbye, my mother wrapped in grief and me in a sort of shocked numbness.

Mum couldn't sleep in her bedroom, so I made up the spare room with clean sheets and tried to settle her there, but she couldn't relax and paced around the house alternating between tears and anger.
Dr Burke had given me a sedative for her and finally after getting her to eat a piece of toast and drinking an umpteenth tea of the day, I managed to get mum to lie on top of the spare room bed, fully clothed but at least resting for a while.

I needed some time to process the situation myself. I obviously couldn't go to work now until after the funeral. Who would we even invite? I wandered into our front room and went to dad's desk. It was locked, of course, but a short hunt for the key in obvious places soon revealed its hiding place. I pushed up the roll top and readied myself to delve into my father's private world.

CHAPTER 3

James McDonald was only 61 years old when he died. He had cancer, he knew about it, but hadn't told me or mum. Why? That was anyone's guess now, I reasoned it was some sort of manly code that he'd learnt during his time in the army.

His private life lived in the roll top desk and was slowly revealing itself to me as I sorted through his paperwork. The letter from the hospital, offering him specialist treatment was filed neatly under medical. There were more letters referring to his condition and his original diagnosis two years earlier. So that was the real reason he had left the army, his failing health. Dr Burke hadn't revealed anything like this to mum and I, but according to the paper trail he had known about dad's condition and had tried to persuade him to try the chemotherapy treatment, which seemed to be having positive results in other patients.

I opened a file marked, household affairs. The house had been purchased in 1958 for the heady sum of £1,899. It looked like the mortgage had been paid off in 1963, the same year he'd bought the car for mum;
he must have come into some money. I made a note to check his bank statements for that year. There were no outstanding debts on the house, so that was a relief. At least I would be able to manage the overheads on my salary and I was sure that mum would get a widow's pension and probably an army pension, that would be something at least. Everything was methodically filed with folders stating the file name, which made my life easy. The bank statements neatly put in monthly order, revealed that

dad had indeed come into money. It appeared to come from a solicitor in Edinburgh, an inheritance.

I stretched out my arms above my head, my back and neck had started to seize up, too much time bent over documents. I'd better go and check on mum, it had been a terrible day and I didn't want her to wake up disorientated and suddenly have to face alone the awful tragedy that had occurred. Once again I was reminded that I had never given much thought to my parents' relationship. It was becoming increasingly clear that I hadn't thought very much about my family at all. Talk about take it all for granted. I knew nothing of my parents' past, how they had met, my relatives in Edinburgh, if I even had any. What kind of idiot was I? Not the inquisitive type obviously. That brought my thoughts back to the responsibility of having to arrange a funeral. Who would I invite?

I climbed the narrow staircase and opened the door to the spare room, it was starting to get dark but I could see mum was still lying quietly, the sedative must have worked. I was glad of that, I wasn't sure how I would cope with my mum if she remained grief stricken. I needed to talk to her and for her to advise me, she had always run the house when dad was away in the army. I knew she would be able to continue once she had come to terms with the new life in front of her. The next few weeks would be difficult, I was aware of that but I felt quite detached, as though this was all happening to somebody else and I was just a distant observer. Would I suddenly be struck by grief like mum? It didn't feel that way, I suppose I had never been that close to dad but still, I would have expected some kind of emotional reaction.

I eventually went back to the desk after making myself a cup of tea and putting together a cheese sandwich, which I carefully placed on a serviette so as not to damage the leather desktop. It had occurred to me that there was probably a will, or at least some paperwork telling me where I may find one. I eventually found it at the back of a drawer, purposely put there so as to be difficult to find should someone decide to nose through dad's things. It felt strange all this need for secrecy when my dad's life appeared so mundane. The will had been drawn up by a solicitor in Caterham the year before, after he had his diagnosis. I scanned it quickly, it was glaringly clear that I had not been included in any way. Everything went to my mother, with a small sum of £100 to an Ester McDonald, whoever she was.

Not even a mention, which was weird. I would have thought that I would have featured somewhere, he could have left the house to me and mum jointly, after all, I would probably have to stay here and look after her. I felt a bit resentful, I don't know why. What was I expecting, *to my ever loving son, David. I leave him half of my estate.*

That would have been nice, at least the sentiment would have made me feel like I was important to him. He knew how close mum and I had always been; he could have trusted me enough to know that I would always look after her.

"What are you doing?" The sound of mum's voice made me jump as though I were guilty of some sneaky crime.

"Nothing, just going through some of dad's paperwork, seeing if there is anything I need to deal with urgently," I fudged.

"I've been thinking, will we be able to stay in the house David?" She looked pale and shaky.

"Don't worry about any of that mum, everything will be okay. You come and sit down, is there anything I can get you? Tea? Maybe a sandwich? You have to eat to keep your strength up." I steered her by the elbow towards the sofa and gently guided her to sit.

"I'm not really hungry. I just feel empty, I suppose I'm in shock." She sat on the sofa wringing her hands together, turning her slim gold wedding ring round and round on her finger.

"Did you know dad was ill? Did he say anything to you?" I thought she must have known something.

"No, he wasn't very good at discussing things with me. But

it was obvious that he had been getting progressively weaker. I tried to get him to tell me what it was and if I could do anything to help, but he just said that there was nothing to worry about. Nothing to worry about and now this!" She gave a little cry of anguish, and I handed her a tissue to wipe the tears that were rolling down her face.

I made a cup of tea for us both and put together a cheese sandwich for her. I'm not very handy in the kitchen, this was usually my mum's terrain. As I was going into the front room there was a tap on the door, our neighbour. An elderly lady, Mrs Smith, who had lost her husband the year before, was standing with a casserole dish in her hands.

"Mrs Smith."

"David, I don't want to intrude at a time like this. I've brought you something to eat. I thought it might help, you know not to have to worry about cooking, and all that." She handed me the dish and a tea towel, it was still hot.

"Thank you, that is very kind of you. I'm sure mum will appreciate your concern and of course the food."

"It's nothing, I understand. It's always such a shock, even if you know that they are sick, you never can prepare yourself for the actual day."

Mum came into the hall behind me, she had heard the doorstep exchange.

"Doreen, thank you for coming round, please come in."

"I don't want to intrude dear, only to help if there is anything I can do?"

"I'm afraid it's a very sad house but please come in. David would you be kind enough to make Mrs Smith a cup of tea?"

Mrs Smith linked my mother's arm and they walked together into the front room. I dutifully went into the kitchen and made yet another cup of tea. I hoped that Mrs Smith might help my mother process some of her heartache as I felt awkward with the emotional aspects of my mum's trauma. Especially, as I still hadn't felt the grief that my mother was clearly feeling.

When I returned with the tea, Mrs Smith had a protective arm around mum's shoulder as she sobbed into a tissue.

"I had no idea he was so ill," she bemoaned.

"Of course not dear, I understand," Mrs Smith soothed, "Men are not good at sharing their emotions. I was in shock when Bill passed away, all of a sudden like. You'll feel better in time, after the funeral, it goes off day by day."

I could see it was this very female sympathy and understanding that my mother really needed. Doreen Smith's shared experience easily trumped my clumsy attempts at empathy. I was glad to escape the oppression of deep mourning and left the women to talk.

Deciding that maybe I needed a stiff drink I poured myself a Glenmorangie from my dad's cabinet in the dining room. It was the first time I had ever had the audacity to help myself to dad's private drinks selection, it was strictly for guests, guests we never seemed to have, and at Christmas and New Year's Eve of course. I kept having these feelings of guilt. The desk, now the drinks cabinet, it made me realise how stiff and old fashioned we were.

The next day, Sunday, passed in quiet introspection. I continued going through my father's affairs and mum moved around the house like a ghost. She didn't question me any further. I knew she would be happy for me to slot right into the role of man of the house. Once she had ascertained that we could just continue as usual she showed no interest in any of the details. Even after I told her that everything had been left to her in the will, except £100 to an Ester McDonald, she didn't seem interested at all. I asked if she knew who she was, maybe a relative? Mum had never heard of an Ester McDonald, as far as she knew dad was an only child, and both his parents dead.

I assumed that the solicitor in the High Street whose stamp was on the will would have contact details. I would need to invite this unidentified woman to the funeral.

On Monday, I telephoned the undertaker and made an appointment for that afternoon. The office of Chappel and Son was all grey and purple upholstered furniture, a dark wooden desk and a glass fronted cabinet containing brochures, all in the same dark wooden hue. A sombrely dressed gentleman, who turned out to be Mr Chappel junior, met us with practiced sobriety. We sat at the desk and chose from the brochure a coffin in light oak, with brass handles.

My parents had never been particularly religious, we were apparently Church of Scotland, but my mum shocked me as she pronounced in a firm voice, "It was my husband's wish to be cremated."

"Of course, Mrs McDonald. We can arrange everything with the crematorium for you. Have you any idea how many may attend the service?"

"Can we tell you later in the week? I have to contact my father's old regiment," I answered for her, seeing that we hadn't discussed the practicalities of the service or any kind of reception afterwards.

"Yes, of course. That's not a problem." Chappel junior was solicitously helpful.

That was my next step. I called Smythe as soon as I had finished with the undertaker and explained what had happened.

"I'm dreadfully sorry old chap. If there is anything I can do please ask."

"Well actually, sir, can you tell me who I should contact from the regiment? I would like to invite some of my father's friends to the funeral."

"Leave that to me, David. I can contact the Colonel in Chief for our division and see who will represent them."

"I appreciate that, thank you. I really didn't know who to speak to about such a thing."

"No, of course not, leave it to me."

I felt relieved, hopefully someone would contact me and let me know who would attend so that I could notify the undertaker. I couldn't imagine how awful it would feel if there was only myself and mum there.

As it turned out mum invited a few of our close neighbours and Smythe some of dad's compatriots from the regiment and the whole affair passed in a dignified blur. I held mum's arm throughout and could feel her silent sobbing through the arm of her black coat. She wore a small hat with a net that obscured the puffiness of her eyes. The night before she had found it hard to control the tears, the funeral and the finality it represented was a huge ordeal for her. I was extremely pleased when the whole thing was over and we could resume our normal lives.

We had spent so many years without my father's presence that it was easy for us to just slot into our own rhythm. I went to work and paid the bills, mum did the shopping and cooking. At the weekend I helped her with the heavy jobs in the garden or fixing minor issues around the house. Anything more and I organised for a professional to come in.

We never did find out who Ester McDonald was. The solicitor didn't have any details only an address that proved to be old. Miss or Mrs McDonald had moved on and nobody appeared to know where to.
I decided that at some point in the future I would visit Scotland myself and see if I could trace this mystery woman and until then, I pretty much forgot about her.

I had considered joining an adult dance group but had never got round to it, but mum stepped out first and joined a local bridge club. I was pleased for her, she needed more company than I could provide. Then something started to change. At first, I was glad that mum had started to look after herself. Trips to the hairdressers and a new hairstyle started the roller coaster. My mum had always been pale, a natural blonde, with regular features, above average height and slim. It had never occurred to me that she was attractive. But before my eyes over the next six months she totally blossomed into an unrecognisable woman. She went to the bridge club three nights a week and joined a book club that she attended once a month at the suggestion of Harry. Then Harry said this, and Harry said that, was threaded through all her conversation. Eventually, I felt it was time to meet this 'Harry.' I suggested a Sunday pub lunch and mum was so excited.

"You will like him David, he's such a laugh. Everybody at the bridge club loves him."

Including you, I thought possessively. But I didn't say anything. I wanted to get the measure of the man first. It wasn't that I didn't want my mother to be happy, I only wanted to protect her. I had assumed that role a long time before my dad died and I wasn't ready to relinquish her, not yet.

The lunch was not a success. I found Harry slightly common and way too familiar with mum and myself. Who the hell did he think he was? I left the pub feeling annoyed and especially because mum had blushed and fawned over his every word. Her infatuation was as clear as day and I wasn't sure he deserved her.

Harry had been married before, twice. He had slick Brylcreemed hair, combed back off his face; I was sure it was dyed as it looked unnaturally black to me. His neatly groomed moustache seemed to be way greyer than the immaculate hair. His face was ruddy and I wasn't surprised as he knocked back a number of double whiskeys. He dressed in a Harris Tweed jacket with military twill trousers and very polished brown brogues. The whole effect screamed contrived.

I eventually got a word in edgeways and asked what regiment he had been in.

"So, Harry, where did you serve?"

"Oh, you know, here and there," he answered evasively.

"Harry was in Intelligence, David. He can't tell you any details, you know how it is."

Yes, I knew how it was, I was pretty sure that Harry had never been in any of her majesty's services. We ate our Sunday roast, it was a busy Carvery pub in Godstone and not bad. I was pleased that queuing to get served at the open kitchen and eating took up some of the time, where too much conversation was unnecessary. I didn't want to be a kill joy but was relieved when the whole ordeal was over and I could make my excuses to leave. Mum and Harry were driving onto Brighton for the remainder of the afternoon so I drove mum's little Morris back to our house in Caterham.

I had managed to whisper a word of caution in her ear before I paid the bill to leave, "He's had quite a lot to drink, are you sure you are okay with this? I can give you a lift home."

"No, don't be silly David, he's only had two whiskeys and he's an excellent driver, he's done rally car racing you know." She smiled indulgently at me as if I was still a child. "I'll be fine, don't worry darling."

But I did worry, and with good reason.

CHAPTER 4

By Easter time, barely six months after my dad died, Harry and my mum had become a recognised couple. And to my absolute horror, he proposed and my mum accepted.

I was stunned as she happily showed me the tiny diamond engagement ring. The .25 carat, set in a plain nine carat band told the whole story. It had never occurred to me, but mum was a catch. She owned her own house, outright, and dad had left a tidy sum in the bank for her care and welfare. I didn't know what to say, but more importantly I could see that this would spell a complete change in my own life.

The biggest problem for me was that I had never seen mum happier, she looked radiant as she buzzed around planning a June wedding. It would only be in a registry office but that was fine for people of their age, she assured me. I buried myself in my work and surreptitiously started looking for a flat to rent in London. Mum seemed to naively believe that I would just continue to live at home after the wedding, but I couldn't tolerate that little cocksure conman. I was sure it would all end in tears but what could I say? I was a young man and should be living my own life, not trying to stop my mum from living hers.

May came and I had found a house share in Dulwich. The recommendation had come from one of my work colleagues, we were in the kitchen making our morning coffees when he approached me. He had heard me mention that I was searching for a flat in London.

"Excuse me for butting in, but I'm looking for somebody to

share the house I live in. The last chap has just moved out and we are searching for a new person."

"I'm Jason," he said holding out his hand for me to shake. "I'm in accounts."

Jason was taller than me, and I'm quite tall at 6'1". He had the look and sound of a public-school boy. There were plenty of those in the Foreign Office, slightly floppy hair that he had to keep pushing back out of his very blue eyes. He oozed confidence and I was sure he would be a hit with the ladies, unlike me.

That evening, instead of taking the 5.38 to Caterham, I took the 5.30 to East Dulwich and a short walk to a Victorian house on East Dulwich Grove. Jason explained on the train journey that the house belonged to his aunt Maud, but that she preferred the country with her dogs and horses. The room on offer was on the first floor, overlooking the street. It was a large double bedroom with a huge old fashioned Victorian wardrobe and a matching bed. There was a small table come desk with an upright wooden chair, on the right hand side of the large sash windows.

"We share facilities I'm afraid," Jason said apologising for the room not being en-suite. "The bathroom is down the hall, my bedroom is on the top floor, in the attic if you like, and Doug, a Scots engineer is at the back of the house."

We went back downstairs where he showed me the none too clean communal kitchen and a very comfortable lounge which I assumed was under my road facing room.

It didn't take me two minutes to decide to take the room, I suppose I had decided before I had even seen it. I was desperate to leave before Harry moved into my dead dad's shoes and home.

"Great, well that's a deal then," said Jason shaking my hand on the transaction. "We share the bills by the way, three way split, is that okay?"

I assured him it was and told him I would move in at the weekend if that was alright with him and Doug.

"Sure thing old man, good to have you onboard. I'm sure you'll fit in just fine."

And that was that, providence had just thrown me a helping hand and I was determined to take it.

"Why David, I don't understand! You don't have to move out." Mum was seriously dismayed when I announced my imminent departure.

"Neither Harry nor I want you to go, there has never been any question about it, this is your home."

"Yes mum, but it's not right for me to share it with you and Harry. I'm a grown man and it's time I started to live my own life. You are going to be busy with your new husband and your life together."

I couldn't help the twinge of bitterness that had crept into my voice.

It was hard enough to accept Harry in my father's place let alone live in the same house as a witness. Thank God I was old enough to move on, I couldn't imagine how terrible it would be if I was still a young boy having to negotiate this minefield of emotions.

"I will visit, you will have my address and you can always phone me at work if you need me. I'll leave you all my contact details so you will be able to get me anytime."

"I'm sorry David that you feel this way, I really thought we could start again, a new little family." Mum stood in front of me wringing her hands together.

For the first time it occurred to me that she may be frightened to be alone with a new husband. There were obvious emotional and physical barriers to overcome. I had no idea about my parents' sex life. This was never, ever going to be a topic of conversation that was going to happen. I didn't know if my mother had slept with Harry, the thought was totally disgusting to me, and I doubted that they had managed to get that intimate. They hadn't been on any overnight trips alone and she was always home by ten o'clock. Not that it had to be dark for sex, but I couldn't see my mum doing that in the back of a car.

"You'll be alright mum, it's a new experience, a new life. It's exciting."
She didn't look sure and started rubbing her cheek, a sure sign she was worried.

"Look you don't have to marry him, it's your choice." I couldn't stop sounding like a petulant child giving ultimatums.

She turned and left the room, but I could hear her crying in the kitchen. Although I felt sorry for her, I couldn't bring myself to go in there. If only she could have chosen somebody more appropriate, things might have been different. I didn't want to be mean, but Harry? It was clear to me that he was an adventurer. I wanted to advise her to keep a strong check on her money but couldn't add insult to injury, on top of leaving and abandoning her to her chosen fate.

A cold frosty atmosphere prevailed in the house. Harry visited on Friday evening after their bridge club and made a plea to me on my mother's behalf.

"Look son, you don't have to leave. Your mum is really upset, me too. We hoped we could all be a family together."
I didn't want to hear it, I felt like punching him in his smug face. I wasn't a violent man and I didn't approve of thuggish behaviour but at that moment I had the most terrible premonition and just knew that this was all going to end badly. I swallowed the unpleasant
taste that Harry left and extended a hand for him to shake.
"It's time I left Harry, it would be helpful to be nearer my work for commuting and I have my own life to consider."
"Yes, but it's a bit sudden like. Do you have to go this weekend? We're not getting married for another three weeks, you could stay till then."

I realised at that moment he thought my leaving could jeopardise his plans. I could tell he didn't care about me, in fact it was better for him to be the only influence over her, I had played right into his hands. But I couldn't sit back and watch the gradual manipulation that I knew would come once he was her husband.

I heard him in the kitchen when I went to go upstairs.

"I tried Harriet, but he wouldn't listen."

Half an hour later I heard the door close and knew he was gone.

I continued with my packing, still determined to leave the next day. I had no choice. It was my mother who had the choice and she had chosen Harry.

CHAPTER 5

Getting to East Dulwich Grove was a mission. I had two quite heavy suitcases and a carrier bag. I'd packed as much as I could, I didn't want to go back anytime soon.

The door was opened by a bleary eyed Jason, even though it was nearly three o'clock.

"Hey man, great to see you. Make yourself at home, Doug and I are wrecked. We had a party last night and well you can see." He pushed open the living room door to reveal a number of bodies still in various states of undress, the smell of stale smoke and spilt booze was sickening.

"I'll catch up with you later," was all he said as he padded off back up the stairs to his den at the top of the house.

I awkwardly managed to drag one of my heavy suitcases up to my room. I was relieved to find it empty. On my way back down to get the second case I saw a large man in boxer shorts effortlessly pick it up and carry it upstairs towards me. He was smiling a wide smile and looked like he could easily could have tossed a caber!

"Doug?"

"Aye, and you're David, I thought I'd help you out. You look like you're struggling." Even though it was almost an insult to my manliness and in particular my puny strength, it was delivered with such good humour that I immediately warmed to the big hairy Scotsman.

"I locked your door last night to keep that lot downstairs out. You want to keep your door locked. Jason's a nightmare for picking up strays." Doug had a rich deep Scottish accent, and it reminded me that I was in fact a Scot, although not this kind of Scot.

"The kitchen's a pigsty but I'll show you where things are. I doubt we'll see Jason till he starts again tonight."

I followed him down to the kitchen, and he was right.

"Is it always like this?" I asked.

"It gets better in the week, but weekends are for partying." He pointed to the kettle. "Get the tea on Davie lad, I'll shift some of the layabouts in there," and he marched back into the front room, threw open the curtains and started clapping his hands.

"Come on you lot, time to fuck off to your own middens!" he shouted, to groans and moaning from still inebriated party goers.

"Get your shit together and get out. Anyone still here in ten minutes is on clean up duty!"

I had found the kettle and washed up two mugs. I was searching in the cupboards when Doug came back.

"That should get rid of them. None of them will want to tidy up this mess. Second top on the right for coffee," he offered watching me searching. "Should be some milk in the fridge."

"I don't know what that wanker Jason would do without me to watch his back, degenerate twat."

I eventually managed to make two coffees, I couldn't find sugar but there was milk in the fridge, though little else on the empty shelves.

A couple of very dishevelled girls wandered into the kitchen looking worse for wear.

"Can we have a glass of water, please?" Panda eyes appealing to our better selves.

"Of course, sweetheart, it's what you need. Next time remember to drink the water before you pass out, you'll feel better for it." Doug found two glasses which he thoughtfully rinsed before filling them from the tap and handing them to the two waifs.

I couldn't resist a smile at the small blond one, even though she looked wrecked. But she smiled back and Doug winked at me.

"Hey, why don't you two help us clean up? I'll get some stuff from the shop and make us all brunch," Doug suggested.

I was sure that these two wasted girls wouldn't be much help but amazingly they both nodded and started loading debris into the bin and glasses into the sink. It was slow work but by the time Doug got back from the local Co-op they had managed to break the back of the mess. I had concentrated on washing up and had been piling things onto the draining board until I ran out of space. Blondie sidled up to me and told me her name was Clare; she lived in Peckham and had a cute South London accent.

"Thank you for helping Clare." I smiled back at her.

"That's alright, didn't want to go straight home anyway," she replied.

"It's a bloody mess, ain't it?"

"Yes, and I wasn't even here to contribute," I added.

"Not sure I was 'ere much meself," she responded with a girly giggle.

Slowly, we made headway. Sharon, Clare's companion was a waitress at the local wine bar and once she got moving was a real asset. She threw open the windows and opened the back door. It was the first time I had noticed the garden. It looked green and well kept. Aunt Maud must employ a gardener, because I doubted that Jason would be doing this in his spare time.

Doug started on the eggs benedict and set up on the patio table outside. He opened a bottle of cheap fizz and when all was ready shouted to his kitchen crew, "Bucks Fizz on the table ladies and gentlemen. Let's eat."

I was really starting to relax and enjoy myself after the shock of finding my new home a wreck. Clare kept smiling at me and Doug gave me a hefty dig with his elbow in my ribs, I doubted if the big fella knew how strong he was. But it was all good humoured and he was a surprisingly good cook. The eggs were perfect, the company good and amazingly by the time Clare and Sharon left, Doug and I both had dates for that evening, to meet in the wine bar where Sharon worked at 10.00pm.

"Not bad for your first day?" Doug ventured as we waved the two girls off. "We've got dates, we ate brunch and the girls did a great job of cleaning up, the place almost looks habitable."

"Thanks. Brunch was good too, not bad at all for day one, and it's not even over," I added.

"Right laddie, I'm going to catch a few hours shut eye before round two. Need to get my strength back for sweet Sharon." And with that he turned and made his way back to his bed.

I was left in the hall to muse over what had just happened. More than in my three years at university, in fact more than in my whole adult life. This was going to be quite an eye opener.

CHAPTER 6

I loved my newfound independence, my house mates were enlightening. I realised that I had been living in some sort of half life and I revelled in the experience of being relieved from my middle class constrictions.

I was never dedicated to my work, but having Jason there made it more tolerable. We had lunch together and travelled home on the same train. Weekends were a blast, I discovered cannabis and well, things seemed much more chilled when you were stoned.
Doug was like the big brother I never had and Jason the naughty instigator. All the bad stuff was down to Jason, all the clean up to Doug.

When it was time for my mum to marry Harry I asked Doug and Jason to the wedding. Jason refused flatly.
"No way brother, it's not a gig for me."
But Doug, sensing that I was in need of some support, volunteered for the ordeal.

We took the train to Caterham and a taxi to the local Registry Office. Mum looked lovely in a sunny yellow matching dress and coat. She smiled at everyone and gave me a big hug, so happy that I hadn't boycotted the event, and I felt like crying for her.
"Keep it together, son," Doug warned when he saw that I was choking up. "Your mum's a grown woman, I'm sure she can handle the little shit."

The reception was a happy affair, all the bridge club and the book club came for the free food and booze. Doug was a rock for me to lean on. I got quite drunk and confessed my darkest fears on the way back to the house in London later that night.

"It's not your decision, or your life laddie," he wisely counselled.

"I know but I feel the hand of doom on my back Doug."
"Well just wait. Who knows how things will work out, but I'm sure you will be there for her if it all goes tits up."

I was so pleased to have found my own freedom, but I couldn't help worrying about mum.

The next couple of weekends passed in a haze of partying and meeting up with Clare; she had become a kind of girlfriend but I knew that it could never develop into anything more. We were from different sides of the planet. I felt guilty about that but what could I do? The sex never developed into anything else, but she was always available at weekends, if I bothered to call her.

It was into July, and holiday season when Jason announced that we were going to Maud's birthday party and could any of us drive.
I volunteered, although Doug had a licence too. Jason said he'd never been sober enough to pass his test and I could believe that.

We hired a car and headed to Oxfordshire. Maud's place was unbelievable, I tried not to be too impressed but it was hard. It was a stately home, twenty bedrooms of 17th century mansion set in acres of pastureland.

We arrived as dusk was falling and were shown to our room by an incredibly old butler who looked like he had come off a Hollywood film set. The party was on Saturday evening. No food had been laid on for us, so we ate at the local pub, had a few beers and settled down for the night. I felt like I was in a dream, it was so surreal. I was yet to meet Maud who was otherwise engaged.

The next morning, I went down to breakfast and still no sign of Maud or Jason. Knowing that he was a late riser I was pleased to meet up with Doug in the dining room. Served by the butler and a maid, it was quite a formal affair. I looked at Doug.

He smiled at me. "It's something else, isn't it?"

"It certainly is. What are we meant to do today?"

"I have no idea, go shooting or riding I expect. What do you think?"

"I have never been in a place like this, Jason gave me no indication that Aunt Maud was an aristocrat."

"Well you could have guessed, he's a bit of a nob himself," Doug commented in his pragmatic Scottish way.

"Hi guys." Jason swanned into the dining room lifting up the silver covers on the platters and helping himself to an enormous breakfast.

"How are you guys doing?"

"You could have warned me wanker," I responded.

"About what?"

"Oh, come on Jason, neither Doug nor I were prepared for this country house set up." Jason obviously hadn't noticed our bewilderment.

"What, this place? It's Maud's place, you'll meet her later at the party. Just chill."

"It's alright for you to be cool, you were expecting this. I'm just a bit overwhelmed,"

"Nonsense, guys. Maud's really cool you'll see later when the other guests arrive." Jason seemed completely sure that this would all work out for us.

"What are we going to do today?" I asked him.

"Do you ride? She has a wonderful stable, an amazing horse woman."

"Of course, she would be," said Doug unimpressed. "Where's the local pub? Can I walk there?"

"Come on lads, don't be silly. It's a great place to unwind, really."

"I would like to try to ride a horse," I offered.

"Have you ridden before old chap?" Jason was smiling.

"Well, no. But I would like to have a go."

"Great, let's go and find you a gentle mount." He laughed.

The day actually passed quite well. I was found a beautiful filly called Sadie and she helped my first attempt at riding to be less than a disaster.

Later, we met up with Doug at the village pub and had lunch. After a nap and a soak in the most enormous bath I had ever seen, I felt quite refreshed and ready to meet our elusive hostess, Maud.

Guests had started to arrive, champagne and hors d'oeuvres were being served by Maud's staff and still she hadn't appeared. Jason seemed perfectly comfortable and was obviously used to this casual approach to a birthday party, but Doug and I were both feeling a bit out of our league.

"What do you make of this Davie boy? Like we're in some fucking period drama, no?"

"I honestly have never been to a place like this before, it's amazing. The artwork alone must be worth a fortune. Aunt Maud must be seriously loaded." It was awesome. I pointed to our house mate. "Jason seems at home. Look at him over there chatting up those debutants." He was merrily flirting with a couple of girls who looked like they could be on the cover of Tattler.

"It's his natural hunting ground, I suppose. It's definitely not for the likes of me." I could tell that Doug felt uncomfortable.

"Hey guys, let me introduce you to Camilla and Emilia." Jason had brought the debs to us.

Emilia was immediately onto Doug. "Oh, Scottish, how wonderful. Do you know the Argyles?" she cooed in her upper crust accent.

"Probably not, unless they come from Aberdeen," Doug retorted caustically.

"Really, I don't know," Emilia gushed. "I've only visited once for a shoot on their estate with daddy; it was great fun."

"I'm sure it was lassie, and I'm quite sure that I wasn't invited."

"Hey man," Jason cautioned. "These girls are protected, know what I mean? They're not used to irony."

"Okay, sorry ladies, my inferiority complex showing there." Doug managed to redeem himself, but honestly it was all wasted on the girls who just smiled vacantly and really didn't understand the sentiment.

After a while I wandered off. It was quite an experience. The people who had seemed so proper when they arrived had started to relax. Even Doug was chilling with Emilie and we still hadn't seen the elusive Maud.

I went upstairs to put my jacket on my bed and noticed the butler taking a bottle of champagne into a room along the corridor and felt compelled to follow him. As he opened the door, I breathed in the strong aroma of cannabis. I poked my head rudely round the door and observed what could have been a Moroccan den. A richly decorated room with oriental rugs covering the floor and tapestries hanging on the walls.

"Who are you?" came from a woman sitting on the floor in the lotus position. "James, leave the champagne and go." She waved away the butler.

"You, young man standing in the doorway staring. Who are you?"

"I'm terribly sorry to disturb you. I'm David, Jason's house mate."

"Curiosity killed the cat David; did you know that?"

"Well, I've heard the expression. I'll leave you, sorry again," I stammered.

"You don't sound like somebody Jason would know," the mystery woman added. "Stay, come closer."
I dutifully obeyed, I felt I had no option. I was clearly in the presence of the lady of the house.

"Close the door, I can't bear to be observed."
I shut the door and approached. I felt like the queen was summonsing me.

"Well, are you enjoying my birthday party David?" she enquired staring directly at me. Maud was quite an unexpected surprise. I had no idea how old she was and I certainly didn't have the balls to ask.

She could have been anything between forty and sixty; in the subdued light and heady environment it was impossible to tell. She had the greenest of eyes, that I couldn't miss, long hair, wavy like the Lady of Shalott in the painting by the English Pre-Raphaelite artist John William Waterhouse.

"Come and sit next to me, let me take a good look at you." It was a command not a gesture.

"Yes, quite handsome in a delicate way. Where are you from?"

"My parents are Scottish madam," I replied formally. "But my mother lives in Caterham, she is newly re-married, my father died last year."

"I see," was all she said.

"I can offer you Lebanese gold or Nepalese black, I also have some Jamaican weed but I wouldn't recommend it." This was all casually mentioned like she was offering me different types of tea to drink.

I must have looked nonplussed because she smiled benevolently at me.

"You do smoke?" she enquired. "I'm sure you can't live with Jason and be a drugs virgin."

"Well, I only moved in a couple of weeks ago, and I must say it's been quite an eye opener."

She nearly choked as she inhaled on her large spliff.

"How funny you are. I think I'm going to like you David, I think I'm going to like you a lot." I didn't quite know what she meant but I smiled as she passed me the spliff. She watched me with amused eyes as I coughed uncontrollably while inhaling the pungent hashish smoke.

But after a few minutes the effect started to hit me and I found myself relaxing and smiling stupidly to myself.

"You have got to be the most interesting person I have ever met," I slurred as I leaned back on the Moroccan cushions next to her.

"Really, that limited so far, you endlessly amuse me David. I'm so glad that Jason brought you here to meet me."

"Well, actually I drove, Jason doesn't have a licence." Somehow that statement felt hilariously funny and I couldn't stop laughing.

"Are you hungry yet?" she enquired.

"Well now you come to mention it, yes, I'm actually starving."

"That's good, let's go downstairs and welcome my special guests. We can find some food and I can introduce you as my new best friend."

"Am I? Your new best friend? That's wonderful, I've only just met you and I've got to say, you are actually amazing."

She laughed and took my arm, her purple and gold kaftan flowing to the floor, "Come on sweet thing, off we go." And she led me back to the party, smiling and introducing me to everyone there. They all seemed to fawn all over her and I thought to myself that it was because she had to be so rich, but soon I noticed plates of white powder going around and the strong smell of cannabis throughout the house.

"Have a line darling, it will pep you up and help you keep going. It's the finest Columbian cocaine. I can assure you you'll be fine."

I didn't need any encouragement and noticed more sharply that people were looking at me and everything around me had suddenly focused in. Jason came across and took a big line from the plate offered to him.

"Jason darling. Thank you so much for bringing me David. I couldn't have wished for a better birthday present." She took Jason's arm and smiled lovingly at him. "He's my favourite David, he's my brother's son you know. I hate my pompous sibling but Jason is a gem."

I noticed Doug in the corner on the sofa with Emilie, he'd obviously gotten over his prejudice. She was sitting on his lap, and he had his hand way up her thigh.

"It looks like the party is beginning to swing darling. I'm going to take David back to my den so that we can continue getting to know each other." She held more tightly onto my arm and I felt myself being steered towards the stairs. "You take care of things darling," she threw back to Jason over her shoulder.

"Of course auntie, you can rely on me." He gave her a mock salute and helped himself to another line of cocaine.

Upstairs in Maud's room she led me to the cushions on the floor and encouraged me to relax. It didn't take much persuasion, I was stoned, high and drunk on champagne. Life looked like it couldn't get better than this. Maud attracted me intensely and I reached across to her and boldly kissed her. I felt more experienced since my recent adventures with my cockney friend but nothing could have prepared me for Maud.

"No dear." She allowed the kiss then placed a warning finger on my chest. "I'm not interested in sex, you have young women for that sport."

I wasn't sure how to react. But Maud was in charge in this house and I just a humble supplicant at her feet.

"Tell me about yourself David. Where you started and how you got to where you are now."

I later realised that cocaine is an instrument of great verbosity, I embarked on my life story which wasn't very interesting and Maud quietly listened, nodding her head every now and again. She didn't interrupt me until I got to the part about not feeling sufficient grief over the death of my father.

"Why do you think you didn't grieve for your father? Do you think it could be because he had been absent for most of your developing childhood?"

She was probably right, how could you cultivate a close relationship with an absent person, one who when he did show up came in the form of a strict disciplinarian. A man emotionally stunted himself.

"Do you know anything about your father's childhood in

Scotland?"

Maud enquired.

"No, nothing. I only realised after he died that I knew absolutely nothing about my parents as people. It was quite a shock to see he'd left £100 to a person called Ester McDonald. The solicitor tried to trace her through her last address but she had left. That's as far as we got."

"How interesting," Maud mused. "We could go to Scotland David; I have a place there."

"Really," I was stunned. "You are a fascinating woman Maud. I feel sure your life story is far more interesting than mine."

"Oh no, it's really not," was all she offered. "Carry on," she prompted, "what happened to your mother?"

I was far more animated in the story of my mother and especially her courtship and subsequent marriage to Harry. It probably helped that we had indulged in another line of cocaine and a spliff of Lebanese gold.

"What makes you think that this Harry chap will be bad for your mother?" Maud was probing to question my assessment of him.

"I don't know, he feels all wrong. I'm sure he's some kind of charlatan who preys on lonely older women."

"How very moral of you David. Did it occur to you that your mother's life had been stifled by your father too?"

"Well not really, she seemed happy enough."

"There you have it, 'seemed happy enough,' the state of limbo that millions of women have to endure."

"Do you think so? Do you think this Harry fellow makes her happy?"

"For now, maybe. Eventually the question will answer itself."

"Now, I'm tired. You go to bed David. You know where your room is do you?"

"Yes, your staff are very helpful."

"Of course, they are paid well," was all Maud said before standing up and walking out.

I was left lying on the cushions watching the door as it closed behind her. It had been the most highly cathartic night of my life. When I eventually found my room in the vast house, I took a long cool shower and then lay on top of the bed to re-play the whole experience in my head.

The next day at breakfast I found myself alone, no Doug and no Jason. The butler from last night was pristine, standing next to the breakfast platters with white cotton gloved hands.

"Can I serve you anything sir?" He lifted the lids for me to see the food that had been prepared. I chose an enormous English breakfast and sat by myself to eat at a table that could have easily accommodated twenty four. I felt totally self-conscious with the butler standing on duty. He didn't appear to be watching me but as soon as my coffee cup emptied he arrived immediately to re-fresh it. I ventured to ask him where the others were.

"Excuse me, do you know where Jason and Doug are? We have to leave today."

"No sir. Probably asleep."

"Oh, I see. Is it okay for me to wander around outside?" I enquired.

"There is a pool at the back of the house sir, if you wanted to swim?"

"I'd love too, it's hot today but I didn't bring any swimwear."

"That's not an issue, Madam's guests often swim naked."

Wandering to the back of the house, I noticed the pool which looked inviting, its cerulean blue tiles shimmering in the sunshine. There was nobody around. I started stripping off my clothes quickly, the water would hide me and the butler had said it was alright. The water was deliciously cool on my body, I had dived straight in, no toe dipping when you were naked in a stranger's house. I'd just come up for air when I heard a loud whistle. Looking up I saw Doug hanging out of the window that overlooked the pool area.

"Hey Davie boy, what are you doing with your todger out?" he called, laughing. "I can see you've made yourself at home here."

"Wait for me, I'm coming down. That looks too good to miss." A few minutes later, Doug came crashing into the pool displacing water with his leap and shattering my peaceful swim. He splashed me in a boisterously childish way then swam off and knocked out a number of lengths effortlessly.

"Did you grow up a fish?" I shouted as he heaved himself up onto the tiled surround and dumped his wet, naked, hairy body onto a lounger by the side of the pool. I was very aware that I didn't match up to the beast laying proudly between Doug's thighs, but it was too late for modesty and I joined him on the next lounger to bask in the sunshine.

I closed my eyes and luxuriated in the newfound feeling of freedom that had so recently opened up in my usually restricted existence.

Had people always been this uninhibited, was it only rich aristocrats that were overly confident about everything? No it couldn't be because Clare was quite uninhibited too, and there was nothing remotely aristocratic about her. While these thoughts ruminated in my mind, I became aware of somebody blocking my sunlight.

"Hello boys, I do hope you are enjoying yourselves."
I sat bolt upright trying to cover myself. Shading my eyes with my other forearm, I looked up into the enigmatic face of Maud.

"I hope you don't mind?" I stammered.

"Why would I? I have been enjoying both your nakedness from my window and decided to take a look up close."
I knew that I had blushed scarlet, I felt so naked and flustered. Yet completely unable to reach for my pants to cover myself for fear of appearing gauche. Doug with the confidence of a man at home in his own body, and why wouldn't he be, it was quite a specimen of maleness, just lay there shamelessly exposed.

"Good morning Maud, thank you for a wonderful party last night and the exceptional hospitality." He was so cool, he would definitely be able to stand in for Sean Connery aka James Bond any time.

Maud's smile was radiant. "What a delightful specimen you are, Doug."

"Well, I have never been called a specimen before, but I'm sure you meant it as a compliment, so I'll take it as such." He smiled right back.

"David and I intend to take a trip to Scotland soon, don't we David?"

"Er, do we?" I was completely bowled over by Maud's remark.

"Yes, David. You must remember we talked about finding your relative Ester McDonald. I'm looking forward to the challenge and the outcome to your mystery." She stood and pulled the white muslin kaftan over her head to reveal her own perfect nakedness, walked like a goddess to the edge of the pool and elegantly dived in.

"What a woman!" Doug had sat up to get a better look. "How did you get on last night?" He winked with a conspirator's inflection.

"It was nothing like that." I tried to look outraged, but it turned into a sort of giggle.

"What do you mean, 'nothing like that'?" Doug turned to face me, probing, his legs falling open to reveal even more of his manhood.

But before I could add anything, Maud had returned. Sparkling water collected in her red hair and on her milky white body.

We both just stared at her.

Jason chose that exact moment to turn up and put us all to shame, with his neo-classical perfect body completely on show. His skin a perfect shade of honey, his dark hair and form resembling a living statue of David.

"So, beautiful," Maud remarked. "I cannot imagine how my disgusting brother and his insipid wife produced such a god."

He bent with absolutely no embarrassment and kissed Maud on the cheek.

"Maud, darling. Always my biggest fan and most precious aunt." Jason was so at ease with himself. It must come from knowing that he was beautiful and charmed.

"What delightful company." Maud clicked her fingers and out of nowhere her butler appeared. Had he been there all along? I didn't know but I felt as though I was living in some D H Lawrence type idyll.

"My sunglasses and hat, and champagne for everyone," she ordered.

"We must all go to Scotland together to search for David's relative. We can stay at my house in Kelso," she announced. I had no idea what I had set off or why she was so keen on finding Ester McDonald. But Maud was a force of nature and we all just nodded and smiled while James, her butler, poured four flutes of chilled champagne and handed them to us.

"To new friendships and adventure," she declared and we all dutifully raised our glasses.

After emptying her glass Maud stood and pulled her transparent kaftan back over her head.

"I'm going," she stated. "I will meet you all in Kelso for the glorious 12th." And with that she left us staring at each other.
It was Jason who spoke first.

"Better get our things together chaps, need to get the hire car back and get home. I have a hot date tonight."

The drive back gave us all time to adjust to the normality of our usual lives. The weekend receding like a dream the further we got from Oxfordshire.

When we arrived home Jason disappeared to get ready for his 'hot date.' Doug and I took a couple of beers outside onto the table and we looked out over the garden in deep contemplation.

"Do you think she meant it?" I asked him.

"I'm sure she did. The question is, do you want to get sucked into this bizarre woman's game?"

"I don't understand." It seemed simple, just a desire to help.

"She's playing with us all. Jason doesn't care, he's used to it. It's part of his own background, but you and I are different stories."

"I'm sorry, I know I'm thick but I still don't understand. What do you mean she's playing with us?"

"Cat and mouse, son. Cat and mouse."

"Do you think she means us harm?"

"No, not actual harm, but is it good to be manipulated like this? We're men," Doug explained simply.

Of course, I hadn't seen it like that. I clearly didn't possess half the male testosterone that Doug had.

"Why would she do that?" I questioned.

"Because she can, power, pure and simple."

"Do you want to go to Scotland?"

"Oh, yes, I'll go. I'm up for the adventure, but I'll not let her rule me. Scotland is home for me, I have a big family in Aberdeen. I'll hang out with them for a few days then drop in on you lot. If you've had enough or feel out of your depth with these English nobs you can come with me, my lot won't mind you."

"It's an unknown world for me, I have lived such a bland life up until I came here. I want to embrace the difference of Jason and Maud's life. It's like I'm in a novel or something."

"That's grand, just don't get yourself drowned. These people are predators, make no mistake. Their families didn't get rich like that by being good people. Taking what they want is in their genes."

Later in the week when I got home from work I found a book had been left on my bed. The Magus, a John Fowles story of psychological manipulation. I had heard of it but never read it. I assumed it had been put there by Doug.

CHAPTER 7

We took the train to Scotland, we'd debated renting a car and decided not to. It was a long and boring journey which seemed to be mostly Yorkshire. We dozed, ate sandwiches and drank beer in the buffet carriage. I tried to concentrate on The Magus, trying to catch the subliminal message that Doug was sending me. It seemed to be beware of rich, eccentric and manipulative people. Maud definitely fitted the bill.

She had communicated about all the travel arrangements with Jason. I only had to book two weeks off work and follow him. Strange to have all the details unknown to me, like a child being taken to a mystery destination by his parents with no say in any of the decisions. Jason was his usual vague self, proclaiming that everything had been taken care of, just the time of our departure was all I had to worry about. Doug had gone his own way, he would call us and drop in when he'd done his own family thing. I wasn't surprised after what he had said about being his own man and not allowing himself to be manipulated. I sort of admired him, but I was so excited about the whole adventure that I couldn't imagine not just conforming to the plan.

The Rolls-Royce Phantom V was waiting at the station in Berwick-upon-Tweed to pick us up and drive us to Kelso. When we finally emerged from our large four-door limousine it was to a beautiful Georgian Mansion on the edge of the town, set in idyllic south Scotland scenery. Rolling hills framed the building giving the impression of privacy. In fact the house was part of a much bigger estate belonging to personal friends of Maud.

Maud had visited as part of a hunting party many years previously and had been so bewitched with the area that she immediately started to look for a retreat of her own. Scales House had been abandoned for some time and was in need of complete renovation, a project that Maud had overseen personally. She had spent a year of her life achieving the restoration of the beautiful building. The house was restored to its former glory and the coach houses that had sat at the back of the building gutted and made into a heated indoor pool area. Every year she tried to spend as much time as possible in her Scottish hideaway.

I was impressed when the door was opened by James, Maud's butler from her Oxfordshire estate. I hadn't expected him to be in situ.

"Hello James, I didn't think you'd be here."

"I'm sure sir, but madam can't be expected to run the house for herself and guests, alone."

"No, clearly."

James arranged for us to be shown to our rooms and the baggage unloaded from the car and brought up to us. It was early evening and still pleasantly warm. I took a shower, put on slacks and a short sleeved shirt and made my way to the ground floor, hoping to find Jason but preferably Maud.

I hadn't spoken to Maud since my trip to Oxford but I'd thought about her a great deal. She was the most unusual person, and I found myself asking Jason questions about her whenever I could get him alone. I felt embarrassed to ask in front of Doug, something about Doug's attitude told me that he wasn't too pleased with this interest of mine, verging on obsession, to know all about her. But no matter how hard I pushed Jason, he never really opened up about any of the details I was eager to learn. Even when I asked how old he thought Maud was, Jason simply replied that gentlemen don't ask ladies those questions and diverted the conversation to something else. So after all this time Maud was still an enigma.

I met James in the hallway with an empty tray.

"They are waiting for you sir, on the patio." He indicated to follow him and we walked to the back of the house through the elegant, yellow hues of the Georgian sitting room and out onto a large patio.

Maud and Jason were sitting, champagne flutes in their hands, heads together smiling as though sharing some secret observation. I don't know why, but I felt a stab of jealousy at their easy intimacy.

I approached slowly and Jason looked up and noticed me almost creeping up on them. He waved and Maud turned to welcome me.

She was more beautiful than I had remembered and now in the soft evening light I could see that she was probably closer to forty than sixty.

"Darling David, you made it, finally. Jason and I have been waiting for you."

I felt the heat that preceded a full-on blush. I hated my pale complexion, my feelings were so transparent.

Maud just smiled and held a bejewelled hand out to me.

"Come and sit next to me, I've missed you both. Jason was just telling me about your boring occupations, what a shame. Why don't you just both quit and come and live with me? It would be such fun."

We didn't get past her throw away remark before I noticed James hovering by the French doors.

"I think James is telling us that dinner is served, Jason was starving so I ordered to eat early. I hope that is alright with you David?"

It would have to be, I could see that Jason would be catered to, as her favourite nephew.

Leaving the patio we wandered into an elaborate dining room. Candelabras were lit and reflecting the sparkling crystal table settings and glasses. It was very atmospheric and I was immediately put in mind of the elegant dining of the Bloomsbury Set. The food and wine were excellent and I began to understand why Maud travelled with her staff.

I was pleased to have studied English Literature at Kent because for once it gave me the upper hand on Jason. My passion had been for 17th and 18th century literature which was the perfect conversational backdrop for a house like this. Especially after I learned that Maud had overseen the renovations herself and had dug deep for authenticity, which happened to include a library. I saw Jason yawn a couple of times and felt ridiculously pleased with myself. I wanted to show off for this woman, I wanted her to be impressed. But even more than that I yearned to become her lover.

Coffees and brandies were served in the library, which was stunning, a monumental collection of first editions. Ceiling to floor, hand picked volumes by the writers I had read and so admired. It only took Jason another half hour before boredom won and he took his leave, kissing his aunt on her cheek and wandering off towards the staircase.

"You are not too tired dear?" Maud enquired.

"No, certainly not. Over stimulated I would say, your library is most impressive. In fact everything about you is impressive." I stopped before I sounded too gushing.

"Sorry, I shouldn't have been so forward. I apologise."

"Never apologise for giving a lady a compliment. It is a rare man who knows how to be charming and honest."

She walked over to a desk that held a beautiful Asian carved box; opening it she took out a pre-rolled joint, put it to her mouth, lit it and inhaled deeply.

"I have many plans for you young men. I have arranged some grouse shooting at a friend's estate, I will supply you with everything you need so don't be anxious. If it's your first time that is wonderful, there has to be a first time for everything and

I'm happy that you are ready to embrace new challenges."
She passed me the joint and my hand brushed against hers. It
sent a tingle right up my arm like an electric shock and I'm sure
that somehow she felt it. I was too much of a coward to attempt
any kind of intimate gesture. She had rejected my clumsy kiss
before at her birthday party, and now I just stared at her doe eyed
as she smiled benevolently at me.

"Relax David, you are tense. Smoke the joint and go to bed, I
will see you tomorrow bright and early for breakfast. Please help
yourself to any of the books that interest you."
She brushed past me and left the room, a cloud of Chanel
hitting my already overloaded senses. I slumped into the leather
Chesterfield and breathed deeply. It was the first time I thought
that maybe I shouldn't be here and that in fact Doug was right, I
was way out of my league.

We set off early, Maud had insisted that I take more than just
a coffee for breakfast.
"You will need sustenance, it's a long time before we break for
lunch and it isn't the 19th century, there won't be staff waiting
on us." She smiled at me. Jason seemed bored, I had begun to
think that he was only here to please his aunt and actually had
no interest in country pursuits.

Maud was right, the hunt was hard. We covered miles of
countryside up and down on foot and didn't stop until around
two, by which time I was starving. The gun and pack that I had
been given was heavy. In fact during the whole day I didn't fire
one round. Maud was in her element and bagged a couple of good
grouse which I was informed would go to her larder to be hung.
Jason also managed a reasonable day without too much sulking;
it was after all something he'd done before so wasn't out of his
comfort zone, like me. By the time we returned to the manor
house I was exhausted. I really hoped I wouldn't have to repeat
this supposedly pleasurable day out. I jumped in the shower and
let myself relax as the water eased out my tired limbs.

Feeling slightly better and certainly refreshed, I went downstairs to the boisterous sound of Jason welcoming Doug in the hallway.

"I got here in the end!" Doug shouted up to me as I descended.

"And not a moment too soon, I'm already saturated in Scottishness," joked Jason, shaking Doug's hand and taking his bag from him. There was no sign of Maud but she must have heard the commotion the re-union was creating.

In the sitting room Jason poured us all a large whiskey.

"The three musketeers, back together again," he toasted.

And we clinked our glasses together to welcome our friend to our Scottish retreat.

"So how are you guys holding up?"

"I'm quite bored," admitted Jason.

"I'm just exhausted, we've been hunting today. I don't think I'm cut out for it."

Doug laughed and clapped me hard on my back in a brotherly gesture.

"Too soft, you're not a real Scot, that's all I can say."

Then like an apparition Maud appeared, head to toe in white silk, her red hair piled on top of her head in a messy chignon. I thought she had never looked more beautiful and gazed at her in open admiration. A look that I'm sure Doug caught as he threw a smile and a slight tick of his head in my direction. Then Doug totally surprised me, or maybe he was just teaching me some kind of manly lesson. He went across to Maud, lifted her hand to his lips and bowed slightly over it, while gazing boldly into her violet eyes.

"Doug, I'm so pleased that you could make our little gathering."

She allowed her hand to linger in his and looked at him in a sensuously inviting way.

"Let's eat," she announced and we followed her into the dining room, which was set for four, even though Doug had only arrived minutes before.

The table sparkled, fine dining was normal around Maud. We drank champagne to welcome Doug and listened to his amusing descriptions of his time in the bosom of his Scottish family. The whole evening seemed to be lifted by his presence and I found myself once more in the grip of some kind of jealous emotion. While I was genuinely happy that he had arrived, there was something in the way he dominated through his male presence, and I watched Maud carefully to see if she was responding as I feared, or if she herself was still in command here.

My close observation hadn't gone unnoticed. When we'd finished eating we went to sit outside on the terrace. It was a beautiful balmy evening with stars blanketing the deep space around us. Maud gently took my hand.

"David, there is no need for sadness. I have some important family news to discuss with you tomorrow. Then on Saturday evening we are invited to a ball, where I am confident your special skills will be unsurpassed."

"What is the news?" I couldn't help but be curious.

"There is time for that in the morning. I know today was not to your liking, and I certainly will not burden you again with this kind of physical pursuit."

"No, it was okay." I didn't want to appear a sissy with the overwhelming male presence of Doug just feet away.

She gave a dry laugh and looked towards Doug. I could tell she knew exactly what my problem was and I felt humiliated by her perception.

"I will retire now, you young men enjoy your own male company without my intrusion. There is cannabis and cocaine in the boxes on the table for your amusement and just help yourself to the bar. I will see you all tomorrow." And with that she left us sitting there.

Jason immediately delved into the engraved smoking box and rolled a huge joint. Very soon we were all smiling together in a stoned companionship. The tension gone with Maud.

The next morning I was anxious to know the meaning behind Maud's announcement. What news could she have for me?
After we'd finished our breakfast I joined her in the library to find out what she'd meant.

"Well David, I do hope you don't mind but I have taken a liberty with your private life." I was still baffled.

"You mentioned in Oxfordshire that you had an unknown relative in Scotland, an Ester McDonald." Maud handed me an A4 manilla envelope.

"It was addressed to me so I read it. I'll go and get a coffee for us both while you read and absorb the information."
Maud returned five minutes later, I had read the contents of the report by then. It was from a private detective agency in Edinburgh, Jessops and Son.

"What do you make of it? Are you okay? You look a bit pale." Maud was observing the emotions as they crossed my face.

"I'm not sure what to say, I have never heard of any of this, I can't believe that it was never discussed. My father had a previous family and a living daughter and said nothing, ever." I took a deep breath.

"Would you mind awfully if I use your phone to call my mother?"

"No, of course not, please do," and she pointed to the phone on the desk but made no effort to leave me to any kind of private conversation.

"Hi mum. It's me David."

"David, I'm so glad you called, I have something important I need to talk to you about but didn't know how to get hold of you."
And before I could impart my news she continued, hardly drawing breath. "It's the house, you see. We want to sell it. Harry has seen a wonderful business opportunity, a great pub in Cobham. It's a perfect place, we've visited twice now and made an offer. We just have to sell the house to pay for it. Harry and I

are so excited. I do hope it will be okay with you?"

Finally she stopped. During the conversation I had sunk onto the chair behind the desk and was nervously running my hand through my hair. Maud was staring at me, she could see I was shocked. Rocking my head from side to side in an attempt to clear my mind. I had known that this would come. I had really wished that I was wrong for my mother's sake but the writing was clearly on the wall.

"It's your house mum, you can do what you want." I couldn't manage anymore, no warnings, no reprisals, no safety net.

"Okay, I'll go then." As an afterthought she added,

"What was your news David?"

"Nothing." And I hung up.

"Oh dear, that looked like very bad news?" Maud was concerned, the apprehension clearly visible on my face.

"I knew he was a charlatan, I just knew it. Harry wants to sell mum's house to buy a pub," I said flatly. "I can tell you now, she will be left high and dry, destitute, and he will be off fleecing some other poor widow."

Maud looked thoughtful. At that moment Jason decided to barge in to see what the plans were for the day.

"Take Doug and go off somewhere, you can take the car. David has had a shock and we are going to see what can be done about it."

"Okay, if you're sure you don't want to join us."

"Quite sure, just go away Jason." She dismissed him like he was a child at boarding school and she a strict teacher.

"Come and sit next to me." I dutifully did what she said. I was more shocked than when my father had died and that thought crossed my mind and seemed to enter hers. Even the news that I had received about Ester McDonald seemed uninteresting now.

"The obvious solution is for you to buy your mother's house." It was a bland statement made by somebody who had unlimited wealth at her disposal.

"And how can I do that on my salary Maud?" I didn't mean to sound so surly and immediately apologised for my rude tone of voice.

"I'm sorry, I shouldn't take it out on you. Of course that would be the perfect solution but it's simply not possible."
Maud picked up my hand and ran her fingers over the back of it, it was a comforting gesture and I felt like crying. Her fingertips softly stroking. She turned fully and drew me to her, my head resting on her breast. She knew that I had lost control of my emotions and that this was because I loved my mother and couldn't bear to see her hurt and abused. But I knew it was coming. I had known from the first time I'd met Harry.

"I will give you a private mortgage, no strings attached. I can have it drawn up by my lawyer. You can pay me back at an affordable rate. Then you will own her house and can be confident that you will be able to protect her in the long run." I pulled away and stared at her.

"You would do this for me?" I couldn't believe what she had just offered.

"I would do anything for you David, you are my special friend. Your motivation is pure and unselfish. I admire your desire to protect your mother from a predator who preys on vulnerable women."

"I wouldn't want her to know it was me who bought the house."

"She wouldn't need to know, I will arrange everything with my people. It can all be done anonymously."

"Won't I have to go and sign the papers? I've never done anything like this before."

"No, don't worry. Now, we have got rid of the other two, so what shall we do together for the day?" She stood and walked to the desk.

"What is the address of your new house? I mean your old house."
I joined her and wrote the information on a piece of paper that she handed me.

"Leave it to me. We have done a good thing today and I feel extremely happy." She smiled indulgently at me.

"Let's go to my bedroom and make love."

I was shaken to the core. She gave a girlish giggle and took my hand again for the second time that day. She could have led me anywhere I was so overwhelmed, by her generosity but also by the power of her sexuality. I knew that I would never meet another woman like Maud. I knew that I loved her completely. What I didn't know was whether that was a good or bad thing.

We spent the rest of the day in bed, she was shameless and beautiful, without any embarrassment or restrictions. I had never considered myself a good lover, but I was consumed by her. I made love to her with every fibre of my being, every inch of her, the most precious gift I had ever known. The bed was trashed, we lay together side by side sweating and sated. I had no words that were good enough, no poetry especially written, no eloquence that could describe what had happened to us. Nothing but a clasped hand.

Suddenly, she jumped out of bed, completely naked and walked to the phone on her dressing table. She made two calls, one to James in the kitchen for champagne, the second to her solicitor, Bryan Hammond.

"Bryan darling. It's Maud. I want to buy a little house in Caterham, Surrey for my friend David McDonald." I was amazed that she could remember the address without referring to the paper downstairs on her desk.

"Yes, yes, don't worry about the money. It won't be much. Just offer the asking price and pay more if there is any competition. We will do it all through your office, he wishes to remain anonymous... Of course I know what I'm doing. There is no need for you to worry darling. David is extremely important to me... No of course I won't marry him." She looked over at me and made a gesture, shaking her head. "I've told you before I will never marry again. Once was most definitely enough."

After a short pause she continued, "Thank you darling, just

sort it out for my friend, he is very anxious to obtain this property. I will explain the next time I'm in London. I'll take you somewhere nice for lunch, you choose." And with that she hung up.

At that moment James knocked and arrived in the room, seemingly oblivious to Maud's nakedness and my presence in her bed. With expert discretion, he placed the tray on a low table and left.

"Well, this has been a most exciting day. You have thoroughly cheered me up. Now you must teach me how to dance like a professional before Saturday night. I will enjoy the shocked expressions of the stuffy boarder crowd at Lord Hartford's ball."

Maud returned to the bed and we made love again. I had never been so physical in my life and I marvelled at my newfound prowess. She had totally turned the tables and now dominated me in the most outrageous way. She rode my slight frame in total abandonment. I was a stallion who she controlled. She laughed and threw her wild hair back over her shoulder, her breasts heaving as she plunged up and down on me. Then the riding became increasingly fast, my whole body being rocked backwards and forwards with the intensity of her grip, her knees bruising my thighs painfully and finally she screamed and collapsed on top of me. I knew that I had not exactly satisfied her, but she had certainly satisfied herself and I felt incredibly proud.

By the time I returned to my room to shower and recover I felt sore and used. Strange, I wasn't expecting such energy or such a violent coupling. After this morning's tenderness this was slightly shocking.
I realised I was a novice where sex was concerned, my feeble attempts with Rachel and my weekend romps with Clare were the sum total of my experience. Maud was not the kind of woman I could even speak to let alone make love to, yet I had.

She seemed to be taken with me, although I got the feeling that I was almost some kind of pet she had acquired and now owned.

When I eventually went downstairs Jason and Doug were sitting with her on the terrace, they were all drinking champagne and laughing. I immediately felt nervous that maybe I was the butt of their joke, because the intimacy that Maud and I had shared that day had disappeared. She was charming towards me of course.

"David darling, sit next to me." She waved me to the rattan chair closest to hers.

"Doug and Jason had quite an adventure in Berwick, you must tell David what you got up to. They are both quite incorrigible."
I couldn't really concentrate on their tale of drunken revelry in a stuffy hotel restaurant over lunch. It seemed childish compared to my day of heightened passion. Still worse was the outrageous way Maud flirted with Doug. Although he batted her advances away with casual indifference, this only seemed to encourage her more.

"I do hope you will wear traditional dress to the ball on Saturday night Doug, I can't wait to see you dressed like a real Scot."
It would have been churlish for me to have reminded her that I was also a real Scot, as she put it.
I felt quite disconcerted, I questioned myself over again and again about my real feelings for Maud, but always came back to the same place. I was in love with her, there was no other reason for the way I felt.

Dinner was a trial and as soon as I could I made my excuses and retired to my room. I needed space to think about everything.
 It was a warm night, my bedroom window opened onto the terrace below. I could hear the others laughing, their happy inebriated voices rising and falling, drifting up accusingly into my solitude.

Was this what literature described as the agony of love? This all consuming jealousy, a sense that I had somehow been used and betrayed. I had to work out a coping strategy and quickly, I was too exposed emotionally. Maud and especially Doug would pick it up easily. I had never been a great actor but I would have to learn how to appear totally relaxed and sophisticated in my new situation. The whole holiday had just become incredibly complicated and a dangerous roller coaster of deception. I had made an enormous mistake in becoming emotionally entangled with Maud.

Over the next few days I made a great effort to practice what I thought of as my inner Noel Coward. I had attempted it a little at university. It was my way of appearing superior and affecting a casual disdainful approach to life. I had imagined that it made me more sophisticated; it probably just made me look ridiculous but at least I wasn't acting like a lovesick schoolboy. I was encouraged and pleased to see Doug rebuff all of Maud's inuendoes and suggestions, but he did allow her to purchase a traditional kilt and accessories for him to wear to the ball, along with formal dinner suits for Jason and me.

There was no repeat of the sexual experience that Maud and I had shared and she acted like she had forgotten all about it. At first I felt hurt, but then I could see that it was all for the best. There was never any future for me with Maud; it was simply the imaginings of an adult fairytale.

After breakfast for the next few days, we practiced our dance moves on the terrace. I was surprised to find that Maud could dance, quite well in fact. A bit rusty but in my experienced hands she soon improved.

"You are a wonderful dancer David. Why on earth did you stop?"

"I'm afraid real life got in the way."

"We must do this more often, I have really enjoyed these lessons."

"I am at your disposal, madam," I responded formally. The act was working. Only the slightest tremor when I first took her hand gave me away and I could see by her face that it pleased her to torture me like this.

CHAPTER 8

Saturday finally arrived, one more week till we all returned to our London lives. Doug was leaving before Jason and me as his two weeks were nearly up and he was due back in his office by Monday morning. He had arranged to take the train from Berwick early on Sunday.

Maud had good news for me, she summoned me to the library to disclose that her agent had made an offer for the house in Caterham of £6,999 and it had been accepted. Maud thought it was a good investment. The agent had instructed her solicitor to draw up the paperwork and when I returned to London I would go to the solicitor's office and sign the agreement.

"Are you sure that you are okay with this Maud?" I tentatively asked.
There had been no repeat of our day of passion, and I really didn't know where I stood.

"Of course darling, I will buy it outright and give you a private mortgage, as agreed. We will both feel better when we know that your mother will be safe regardless of her choice of husband."

"I cannot tell you how grateful I am Maud." I looked meaningfully at her, trying to convey more than just my gratitude for the private mortgage.

"Will you ever tell her about Ester McDonald, David?"

"I'm not sure. I don't really want to speak to her. I'm not sure that I can control my anger at her naivety."

"It is not for you to be angry David, don't waste your emotions on dilemmas that you cannot control."

I felt like this remark was aimed at more that just my mother's situation, it could just as easily apply to me and Maud. I was becoming increasingly aware that Maud played with people. It was a kind of hobby, she exercised control over her players for fun. I had to learn how to deal with it if I wanted to remain in the game. And I did want to keep playing her game. I couldn't imagine how dull life would be now, without Maud.

That evening we were easily the most beautiful and sophisticated group at Lord Hartford's ball to kick off the hunting season. We were announced as we entered the magnificent 18[Th] century mansion as Madam Maud Shafer and guests. We were shown through to the ballroom and right away I elegantly took her hand in my most professional fashion and led her to the dance floor. We danced the waltz in a seemingly effortless glide, our heads and shoulders placed at the most perfect angle, our practiced footwork more than impressive. There was even clapping when we finally stepped to the side of the ballroom to take our refreshments.

"That was amazing, wonderful. Thank you so much David!" She exclaimed with a little clap of her gloved hands.

I bowed slightly; in this environment I was king and I knew it.

I was immediately assailed by ladies all wanting to dance with me, I could see Maud's amused face as she chatted and flirted with Doug. Every now and then winking at me, as if sharing some secret knowledge that only we were aware of.

Doug and Jason were both equally impressive, Doug in his red and black Highland Tartan looked most handsome and Jason in his black dinner suit. His chiselled, handsome dark looks were receiving admiring glances from many of the ladies. Maud was surrounded by her followers and was in her element.

We left just before twelve, the whole evening a whirlwind success, ending with more drinks on the terrace when we returned, more cannabis and lots of joking and laughter. Finally disappearing into our solitary sleeping quarters.

I lay awake for what seemed like hours, I was hot and aroused. Desperate to visit Maud, to relieve some of my pent up passion but more to be re-assured that I was still somehow desirable to her.

Doug was up early the next day and we all assembled in the hallway to say goodbye. I had the strongest feeling that I should leave with him, but it seemed rude to bail out after only one week, especially when I was so beholden to Maud for helping me with my mother's situation. I didn't understand why Maud was so distant, yet not. I suppose I had thought that an affair was just that, a two way engagement. After the afternoon we'd spent together I wanted more
and Maud was like a kind aunt, not a lover. I didn't know how to process any of it, what did she want from me?

We had been invited to lunch with the owner of the whole estate, the Honourable Stephen Fortescue and his wife Camilla. Maud had ordered a taxi to take Doug to Berwick station for the 10.48 to London. Maud had kissed him on both cheeks and looked upset that he was leaving. I had to admit that he was a personality that brought a certain harmony to situations. He was always in command just by his bearing and seemed infinitely more grown up than me in every sense. And Jason, a posh public school boy, selfish and arrogant but so beautiful it just didn't matter.

The lunch was an elegant affair, we sat in the huge 18th Century dining room, the table set with Royal Staffordshire porcelain and silver cutlery. Maud was placed on my right hand side and Camilla Fortescue on my left. Jason was opposite, seated in the middle of the two quite plain Fortescue girls, Jennifer and Grace. Both kept giving him embarrassed sideways glances throughout the meal, neither one bold enough to do anything except answer his polite questions with any more than monosyllables.

As it turned out it was me who was the object of the invitation. The Fortescue daughters were getting ready for their debutant's season and were in need of some formal dance lessons. My debut at the ball over the weekend apparently was the talk of the county, and young ladies were queuing up to acquire such impressive skills. Maud was delighted and happily accepted on my behalf before any consultation could take place. That left me feeling increasingly like some kind of pet or worse still a valued member of staff. But as I was discovering daily, I didn't have the guts to challenge or reject Maud's decisions, my sense of autonomy had almost completely collapsed.

It was decided that I could give the Fortescue girls morning lessons up until the end of the week, that should be enough for them to appear proficient. I would be collected at 9.00am and was of course welcome to stay for lunch if I had no other plans. Camilla hoped that I could help her as well if it wasn't too much of an imposition and she kept sending me sly smiles, which I couldn't help but politely return.

I insisted that I would enjoy the walk up to Silcott Hall in the mornings, that a car wasn't necessary. I consoled myself that these morning lessons would make the time pass more rapidly, until I could escape back to the reality of my own London life.

"Thank you David, we all appreciate the opportunity to be tutored by a professional dancer. Maud has told us that you studied at the famous Frank and Peggy Spencer Dance School and danced with their formation team." Camilla's admiration increased my sense of self worth, which had taken a beating since starting my relationship with Maud. If you could call it a relationship, it was certainly one sided, that was more than evident.

"There, you see. There is absolutely no need for you to continue in that awful job, that you hate David. You have a desirable and valuable skill." Maud took my hand and gave it a small kiss in a very proprietary fashion. I felt sure that it was done for Camilla's benefit, and Camilla immediately picked up on Maud's rather indiscreet revelation.

"But of course David should be teaching dance," Camilla piped up, "it's such an important skill. I can't imagine why you would want to work at anything else."

It stuck me that these rich women had no idea that there was such a thing as having no money. Born rich, lived rich, died rich. Doing more of less nothing useful in the interim. Maybe that was too cynical, but I began to see that as long as you knew the 'right people' there was a living to be made out of teaching people to dance.

During the lunch Stephen Fortescue pretty much ignored the conversation and didn't perk up until Jason started to talk about horses. They disappeared as we took coffee on the veranda and went to look at a newly acquired addition to Stephen's impressive stable. Maud was also interested and invited herself along leaving me with Camilla, Jennifer and Grace.

"Maud's right, of course David. But I suspect that Maud is usually right," she added. "There is definitely a shortage of professional male dancers to give our girls the confidence they need, to go out into the season prepared."

It crossed my mind that these girls only needed money and a family name to attract the kind of husbands that hunted in those circles. Dancing was probably not really on the list of achievements necessary to breed appropriately.

We discussed a few practical considerations, like good footwear and what kind of dance steps they would need. We didn't have time for too much but could probably get a passable waltz and quick step under their belts.

Camilla made it very clear that she was interested in me for more reasons than to learn to dance and while I was flattered by her imperious flirtation, it was also slightly alarming. I hoped that Maud didn't think that I could be pimped out to her socialite friends.

The horse lovers finally returned and saved me from Camilla's increasing advances. Jason would come back later to ride, I wasn't needed till the next day for the morning class.

After Jason left to return to the hall, James found me in my room to tell me that Madam wanted to talk to me in the library. I went, wondering if there had been more developments in the purchase of my house. It felt strange that I had started to think of it as my house, all my life it had been my mother's house. I couldn't imagine such a genteel lady running a pub but presumably she was changing under Harry's tutorage.

Maud was sitting on the Chesterfield, her feet up, a glass of wine in her hand.

"David, darling, come and rub my shoulders, I have such tension since spending time with Stephen and Camilla. She so obviously fancied you. You noticed I suppose, she couldn't keep her eyes off you. I'm sure she would have taken you right there and then if Stephen and the girls weren't there."

I went and stood behind her and dutifully rubbed at her tense shoulders. I didn't bother to deny Camilla's flirtation as it seemed to have piqued Maud's senses.

After just a few moments she grabbed my hand and pulled it over her shoulder to her breast. The effect was immediate and my determination to be cool completely dissolved. I leant across her and caressed her breast while kissing her earlobes and nuzzling like the pet I was, into her neck.

"Let's go upstairs and fool around," she tantalized, and I followed her like a lamb to the slaughter.

Maud quickly pulled off her summer dress to reveal that she had been naked underneath throughout lunch. She pulled the pins from her hair and drew me to her. Then she fell on her knees and buried her face in my swollen groin, while undoing my trousers and releasing my erect member. Slowly she circled the head with the tip of her tongue while looking me directly in the eyes. I was lost, I had no reserve strength to call on, no defence against this siren. Whenever she called. I was doomed to a life of servitude, I could see that now. I allowed myself to be dominated in the way of any true supplicant. Totally, completely.

When she had finished with me I was dismissed. It wasn't cruel, it could have been, there was no lying in each other's arms, no talk of love.

"Go and get washed up darling, we can all go out this evening for dinner. There is a restaurant I like in Kelso. I'm sure Jason will be back soon and will be full of horse talk."

She went to her bathroom without a backward glance, I bent and retrieved my clothes from the floor and went quickly to my own room. No illusions, no pretence, I had been bought and paid for. How many women must feel like this every day, that they lived with partners who didn't love them, just needed their services. But I would leave soon and it would all be over, or would it?

CHAPTER 9

I didn't know it then, but this was the day that was pivotal in changing my life.

It was a warm morning, I was up early and took a quick breakfast on the terrace, a couple of buttered croissants and a coffee.
The walk up to Sillcott Hall was good for me, it helped clear my mind as I tried to look at Maud in a more detached light. The beautiful Scottish lowlands bathed in August morning sunshine, the fields surrounding the estate, a golden hue. Small insects buzzing in and out busily making the most of the glorious end of summer.

I arrived at the hall, humming to myself, the woes of my pathetic infatuation with Maud subsided slightly. So what if I was her love slave? It had to be better than being nobody and I had to keep in mind that she was in effect saving my mother from looming destitution. I couldn't even bear to think about my mum and Harry together, doing the things that I got up to with Maud. It was a sickening thought that I firmly put out of my mind.

The Fortescue women were waiting for me. I was shown into a room cleared of all furniture. It was a large space that apparently had been a music room, but as none of them were slightly musical it would now become the dancing lesson room. I unpacked a small rucksack and removed a pair of shiny black dancing shoes. I had a preference when dancing to wear black trousers and a white shirt, it felt more appropriate.

"Jennifer, shall we start?"

She gave a giggle to her sister and mother who were seated along one of the walls to watch.

I took her firmly by the waist and outstretched my left hand for the lead hold. She giggled again.

"You must try to be serious or we will get nowhere," I admonished.

But I wanted her to relax and follow me so I smiled reassuringly, cued her mother to start the record I had selected, a slow waltz, and started to count the steps to the music, tuning her with my body to follow the steps.

To my surprise she was actually quite good, light footed which helped. We continued the tuition for another half hour, by which time she had relaxed and was actually smiling and moving quite fluidly. I eventually escorted her to the side and held out my hand to Grace.

Jennifer still quite flushed but smiling with excitement dropped into the seat beside her proud mother.

As I escorted Grace to the middle of the floor I could hear her say to her mother, "Marvellous mummy, he's just wonderful."

I felt elated, justified. I might be inferior in every way to Doug's manliness and Jason's beauty but I could dance, and right now that was all that counted. By the time I had finished with the three Fortescues they had all progressed, felt much more confident and were smiling broadly.

"Don't go just yet." Camilla was still flushed from her lesson.

"Come and have a drink with us, you don't have to rush back to Maud?"

"No, of course not. I'm only her guest for the holidays."

I felt slightly indignant and a bit guilty. Was it so obvious that Maud had brought me here for different motives?

"Yes, of course."

We all went and sat on the terrace, there was no sign of Stephen Fortescue and Camilla explained he had gone to Edinburgh. No interest in women's things, she tried to justify her husband's absence but I got the feeling she was happy to be rid of him.

I was expecting tea or coffee but champagne was ordered and opened by their butler.

"Let's celebrate." Camilla raised her glass. "To the wonderful David, come delightfully into our lives to help us in our time of need."

It was a bit dramatic and certainly not true, but I felt myself basking in the blatant flattery. It was certainly helping to reflate my very deflated ego.

They all raised their glasses again and toasted me. I could see that the champagne wouldn't last long and reminded myself to stay sober and not let myself and my newfound status as a hero be tarnished by not being able to hold my drink. I wisely made an excuse to leave after an hour of praise from Camilla and her two daughters. I was pleased that they hadn't left me alone with Camilla, I felt sure she would have made a pass at me and I didn't want to get into a situation like that and mess things up.

I walked back to the manor house on air, still humming the slow waltz by Debussy that had been the backdrop to my first day. My newfound role as a dancing instructor to the minor aristocracy.

Jason and Maud were picking at their lunch on the terrace, talking about horses.

"You look extremely pleased with yourself." Maud observed my silly grin.

"I have had a very successful first lesson with the Fortescue ladies."

"Really, and that old hag Camilla didn't try to seduce you?" She smiled at him and winked. "Come on, I bet she tried to get you alone."

"Not at all, it was all extremely professional."

"I'm impressed David, you see I told you that you were in the wrong profession. We need to send them a bill, a big bill. After all, there are three of them."

"I thought you had offered my services for free Maud." I felt a bit nonplussed at the thought of presenting them with a bill.

"Nothing is for free darling, we all know that," she said coquettishly.

"Yes, of course you must charge them David, they are enormously rich." Jason looked deadly serious. "I reckon for the three of them, at least £500."

"My God Jason, that is an enormous amount." I was shocked.

"Only to you, David. Not them," Jason assured me. "Old Fortescue was bragging he'd just spent over £1000 on a horse. It didn't look worth it to me; the Grey, Maud, you saw it."

"No, certainly, not more than £500 at the most. He was ripped off," Maud agreed with him.

The numbers they bandied around so casually were eyewatering to me. I couldn't charge the Fortescues that kind of money even if Stephen had overpaid for the horse. It seemed obscene.

After a short time the subject was dropped to my relief, I could never tell if they were playing with me or not. Both Maud and Jason had a very different way of looking at things and I always felt like a gauche outsider in their over privileged world.

The very next day at the hall, I was surprised when Stephen Fortescue called me into his library just before I departed.

"Ah, David there you are, do you want a brandy old chap?" he glanced at me, inviting me to take a chair opposite him as he seated himself back behind the large leather topped desk. The brandy decanter was already open on his desk and two crystal glasses next to it. He handed me a generous measure. It was too early in the day to be drinking brandy, but I accepted and just sipped the potent liquid.

He opened the top drawer and handed me a large piece of paper. It looked like a cheque. When I saw it was made out to me for the sum of £300 I was shocked. Had Maud phoned and said something?

"Just something for teaching the girls to dance. I have to tell you I would pay twice that much just to get them to shut up about it," he bellowed in his exaggerated upper class voice.

"But the girls have to find husbands and they have a great deal of competition this year. Camilla assures me you're worth it, shame you can't stay longer. What did you say you did for a living?"

I'm sure I hadn't told him anything, he had been decidedly uninterested in me at the Sunday lunch we'd attended with Maud.

"I work at the Foreign Office, nothing special, just a clerk," I offered.

"I know a few chaps there, take a few more weeks. Camilla will be thrilled and she's the boss here if you hadn't guessed." He laughed at his own joke.

"I'm not sure that is possible." These people had no idea what it was like to have to earn a living.

"Leave it with me. If Maud leaves, you can stay here, we have a few spare rooms. I'm sure the ladies will be queuing up for dance classes." I could see he'd reached his limit with this conversation. "Right, now that's settled, off you go, I'm busy." And with that, I was dismissed. What had happened? I couldn't have told you. I was finding my life increasingly out of my control.

When I got back to the hall, Maud was waiting for me.

"Well, did the old man pay you?" When I nodded she clapped her hands. "Excellent!"

"What did you say Maud? Were you behind the payment?"

"I told him you were worth it. That's all. How much did he give you?"

She was smiling like the cat who'd drunk the cream and I felt that it was much more than that. I took out the cheque and gave it to her.

"Good, you see. I told you that you had a future outside of that boring office job."

"I'm not sure that I can live on that indefinitely," I joked.

"It's the start David, the start of something exciting. You have a real talent and surprisingly, because I know you don't understand your appeal, it's not just for dancing."

She took my hand like I was a child and walked me through to the terrace. Jason was sitting reading the newspaper.

"He paid him," she announced.

"Wow, you are a card Maud. How much old chap?"

"Three hundred," Maud replied before I had a chance.

"But that is only for the one week's tuition surely, for the three women, £100 each. That is more than fair." Jason was way more calculating than I would have thought.

"Well, well. This is the start of something exciting," he said echoing his aunt's words.

I had the strangest feeling that I was a rabbit caught in some kind of snare.

The rest of the week I dutifully presented myself at the hall for the Fortescue ladies dancing lessons. By Friday we had made excellent progress and could waltz with some competence around the music room. The quick step was taking longer and I doubted that there would be time to improve much before I returned to London. For all Stephen Fortescue's assurances that I would be able to take more time off, I had heard nothing and wasn't audacious enough to request this myself.

Then on Friday evening I had a call from Doug.

"You've got trouble brewing laddie."

"What's wrong Doug?" I thought that Jason had spilled the beans on my dancing lessons and that for some reason Doug didn't approve.

"I'm just warning you like. I heard from Sharon that Clare's in trouble."

"What do you mean?"

"Don't be dumb. Trouble, there is only one kind of trouble that occurs when you've been sleeping with a girl, David."

I felt mean but it crossed my mind that it may not be mine.

I assured Doug that we would be back by Sunday and that I would take care of things. Thinking all the time that I would have to spend my dancing money to bail me out of this tight corner and feeling slightly resentful. The last thing I wanted was to be tied to Clare, but really that just made me a selfish bastard, and I wasn't happy with that assessment of myself. I had been enjoying being the hero and now I realised just how vain and vacuous I was becoming.

I didn't want to share this news with Maud and Jason. I knew instinctively that they would just brush it off, tell me I was stupid to feel responsible for a tart like Clare. Imply that it was somehow her fault exclusively and I couldn't face their contempt or, in reality, my reduction in their eyes. I lied and told them my mother was ill, I would leave the next day. Maud was clearly annoyed by this, I didn't understand her at all. But then I didn't understand myself, except I knew that I was a coward.

The next day I walked first thing up the path to the Hall. I was met by an excited Camilla.

"David darling, you can stay. I'm so excited. Stephen talked to some friend at the Foreign Office and he said it would be no problem, you wouldn't be missed. Isn't it wonderful? We're all so ecstatic . We can master the quickstep now," she gushed, her face flushed with the news.

"I'm sorry Camilla, I can't stay. I've had some bad news and have to get back today." She looked horrified.

"No, you can't leave now, what on earth has happened? Can't we sort it out?"

"Not from here, I have to get back to London."
She grabbed hold of me and hung onto my neck like a rejected lover. I was shocked. "No, I can't bear it!" she wailed.

"Camilla please, get a grip. It's alright. I can come back when I've sorted things out."
I looked for assistance but there was none. Then suddenly to my relief, Stephen arrived in the hallway to witness his wife's

behaviour and my obvious distress.

"Put the young man down, Camilla. What on earth is wrong here?"

He actually didn't look too bothered that his wife of twenty five years was clinging to a man in their hallway.

"He has to leave Stephen, some problem in London."

I tried to take her hands gently from around my neck but she just hung on tighter. "No Stephen, NO!"

I looked over her head to her husband appealing for help, my hands open in an attempt to show him that it wasn't me who was holding onto her. But he knew.

"Come on Camilla, old girl." He came and tried to prise her hands from my neck.

"You don't understand Stephen, we can't stop now, we are making such progress. The girls will be devastated."

"Go to the London house. When David has sorted out his private business he can give you lessons there. You can do some shopping, buy yourself something nice." He winked and nodded to me, a conspirator's smile, suggesting that he had pressed the right button.

"Yes! Yes, what a good idea, this is why I love you. You're always so clever, my darling." She let go of me immediately and attached herself to her husband, in a complete about face.

Stephen persuaded Camilla to find Jennifer and Grace and tell them that they had a set back, but that they would go to London and continue their lessons while spending huge sums of money in Harrods.

"I know how to keep my women under control," he pointed to his study. "Leave me your contact details and get away quick, before the other two arrive."

He handed me a card with their Belgravia address and telephone number.

"Let me know what this nonsense will cost me and I'll send you a cheque."

I left the house in a state of mild shock. What was wrong with these people? I had never seen anything like this till I met Maud. Now it seemed like the whole world was mad.

When I got back to the manor, Maud was nowhere to be seen. Jason too seemed to have been spirited away. James the butler told me that a taxi would take me to Berwick. There was a train at 14.30. I thanked him and asked him to make my apologies to Maud for leaving without saying goodbye and properly thanking her for her hospitality.

CHAPTER 10

I finally arrived in East Dulwich Grove at 10.00pm. I was tired but had time on the long train journey to ponder my lucky escape from Scotland. Now I was back, I could end the whole experience. At least from here I was in control again. I tried to convince myself that was true.

Doug was relaxing on the sofa watching television, his feet up on the coffee table, empty beer bottles and the remains of an Indian takeaway strewn around.

"They let you go then. I thought I may have to come back and break you out."

"I lied, I told them my mum was sick. Maud wasn't happy and didn't even give me the chance to say goodbye in person." I slumped into the adjacent armchair, exhausted physically and emotionally. Relieved to be in the sane presence of Doug.

"I spoke to Jason, he told me you were in great demand for dancing lessons, that you had made a killing out of the Fortescues."

"£300," I replied.

"What for dancing lessons? You sure you haven't turned into some kind of gigolo?"

"I'm not exactly sure, to be honest. I've never seen anything like these rich women. Frankly, I'm shocked."

Doug laughed at this. He went to the fridge and came back with two cold beers.

"Tell uncle Doug all about it son."

And I did, I left nothing out. The house purchase, the sex, the crazy Fortescue women. Maud's controlling behaviour. Two more beers each before I'd exhausted my woeful tale. Speaking out loud made it all sound horrendous, I seemed like a naïve idiot and the women predatory animals.

"I'll call Clare tomorrow and give her money to sort things out. The dancing lessons can pay for it."

"Make sure you are responsible first. You never know, and there's no contract between the pair of you. Like me and Sharon, just a bit of fun now and then."

I dreaded facing Clare. I arranged to meet in Dulwich Park, not considering that it was difficult for her to get there from North Peckham. I waited in the tearoom in the middle of the park. It was another nice day, Sunday. I underestimated how busy the place would be with families picnicking in the afternoon sunshine.

Clare was late and I'd almost given up; a feeling of relief spread as I thought that maybe she was too angry with me to meet up. But then I saw her come to the door, eyes searching for me. I gave a feeble wave and she joined me, she looked small and very young and very shy. I felt like an awful cad. My recent adventures had somehow taken me beyond this poor girl.

I had been grateful when I'd first met her, she had definitely held the upper hand. I was woefully inexperienced and she clearly had had many more previous sexual encounters than me. She pretty much led the whole affair and it was fun, easy, no embarrassment or feeling inadequate. Her young nubile body bouncing up and down on mine was all I needed, until I experienced Maud.

Now, it filled me with horror, the thought of doing the decent thing and making her my wife. I knew I was a snob, but how could I introduce Clare to my newfound social circle? The thought of Clare being introduced to Camilla, Jennifer and Grace was ridiculous, let alone Maud.

No, it would have to end today. Here and now. A public setting so that we could maintain some kind of normality throughout. I couldn't face any emotional scenes.

"Would you like something to drink?" I enquired politely. My voice had become much posher since rubbing shoulders with my new entitled friends.

"No, thank you. Maybe an ice cream?"

"Yes, of course." I went to the counter and bought her a ninety-nine, with the Cadbury's Flake stuck in the side.

She sat like a twelve year old with the ice-cream, licking around the edges so that it didn't drop on her summer dress.

"Clare, we have to talk about the situation."

"I know, it's why I'm here."

"Yes, exactly. Are you sure?"

"Yes, I've done a test."

"But are you sure it's, er, me?"

The look she gave me was withering, no more innocent child, pure South London council estate.

"You are a fucking bastard!" She got to stand up and I grabbed her wrist and held her in her seat.

"Please, I'm sorry. I had to ask. You have to see that."

"You think I'm a little slag because I'm common. I hate you. I should never have slept with you in the first place, Sharon told me not to.

She said you were just a stuck up snob like Jason. He wouldn't even shag me and believe me I offered it to him enough times."

That shut me up. I had intended to try to placate her but I felt put down, in my place, which wasn't very high in her estimation. I had just been a poor substitute after a drunken party, and it didn't do much for my self esteem.

We sat in awkward silence for a while; she finished her 99. She had a spot of ice-cream on her nose and I leaned across to wipe it off. She intercepted my hand and held it to her mouth. An intimate gesture not in keeping with her previous attitude towards me, but I didn't pull it away.

"I do like you Dave, I'm not sure that I want to get rid of this baby."

I pulled my hand away, not happy with where this conversation was going.

"I'm sorry Clare, but I'm not ready to make any long term commitments."

"There you go again, you are such a dick, Dave. I don't want a long term commitment, as you put it. You sound like my fucking English teacher at school. Just a bit better looking."

"I don't understand, why would you want to keep the baby if you don't want to marry me?"

"You wouldn't marry the likes of me, come on admit it. You didn't come here to get on your knees and propose, did you?"
I couldn't deny it, it was true. I fiddled with my cup and saucer, not wanting to make eye contact.

"You want me to get rid of it, don't you?"
I begged her not to think like that, as usual my whole handling of the situation had gone wrong. What was it with me and women? They just walked all over me. I was weak, weak and ineffectual. I didn't want to even think of this girl bringing up my child on the North Peckham Estate. It was not how I had visualised my children living. In fact I hadn't even thought about being a parent, I was only twenty-two. I suppose my only experience of family living was my own upbringing and that had been traditional, safe, comfortable, middle class, nothing like Clare's reality.

"I don't think it's a good idea Clare. Think about your future, your own life."

"I'm going Dave, you're an idiot. You have no idea how people live. The gulf between us is too big. I don't want to be like you. If I have this baby the council will give me a flat, I can get money for both of us. Then I can have my own life, no more living in that shit hole with my mum and her fella. I will be better off." She stood up.

"One last thing Dave, I'll need some cash to get started. I'll let you know how much when I get sorted."

She walked away from the café, young and brave. Going off to face a hostile world dressed in an armour acquired on the mean London streets.

I walked through the park back to East Dulwich Grove. I felt defeated, trapped, at the mercy of a woman who I didn't understand. I had stupidly thought that worst case she would beg me to marry her, and at best I would be able to pay for an abortion and learn from my mistake. Neither scenario had happened. She had called me an idiot more than once, and she was right.

I could hear football on the TV. Doug looked up when I entered the room.

"Shit, what happened? You look terrible."

"I'm a moron, an idiot. Not fit to call myself a man," I declared.

"You didn't ask her to marry you? For Christ's sake man!"

"No don't worry. She didn't want to marry a dick head like me."

"Well that's okay then, you're off the hook." It was simple to Doug.

After I had explained what had occurred in the park he was not so blasé.

"Not off the hook, then. More likely on a much more serious hook than before." Doug looked thoughtful.

"Let's have a beer and think about all this, we'll come up with something. I'm still seeing Sharon, I'll be able to keep you informed as to what Clare decides and what happens."

"What's wrong with me Doug? Why can't I control women? Even that fool Stephen Fortescue can manage his, albeit with money."

"You're too soft laddie. Never had enough real men in your life. Your dad was mostly absent as far as I can tell and your mum was a kind pushover. What can you expect? Clare hasn't had your soft upbringing, she is way more ruthless. And Maud, she has had a hard time and that has toughened her right up."

That caught my attention, Doug seemed to know more about Maud's previous life than I did. Why didn't that surprise me? I couldn't leave it, I had to find out what he knew about her.

"You don't want to know, son."

"Yes, I do. I need to understand some of what totally confuses me. Why I am so out of my depth with women?"

It took some telling and he was right, I probably shouldn't have asked but it helped me understand Maud a little better.

Doug had gone skiing in the exclusive Swiss resort of Verbier last Christmas with Jason, he had met Maud and a crowd of her friends there. She had toyed with him, but this is Doug. He didn't let her walk all over him. He fucked her hard during après ski and left. She immediately responded by being overly accommodating. She sent him expensive presents, ripped up his rental contract, so that subsequently he lived in East Dulwich Grove for free. More importantly she told him how she had acquired her vast wealth and it wasn't a pleasant story.

Maud had come from a good family herself; she and her brother had attended expensive boarding schools, owned ponies, played tennis and hung out with the traditional English country set. It's why she knew how to hunt, ride, ski, play the piano and all the skills that it was considered appropriate for young people of quality to acquire.
At eighteen she was bundled off to Switzerland to a finishing school. This was to prepare her for the life of a pampered socialite.

It didn't work out like that. She met a German industrialist thirty years her senior and within a year was married. Her marriage was a nightmare. She was abused frequently, with no way of telling anyone and no means of escape. For five years she lived in purgatory, alone, terrified of her husband and despairing of her life. Then fate threw her a chance. Her husband suffered a heart attack in their private bathroom after a particularly violent sex session. She could have helped him, called for staff or an ambulance but she didn't. She stood in the doorway for hours watching him die, he begged her to help him but she wouldn't. She had no remorse, only overwhelming relief that it was finally over. She sold all his property as quickly as she could and liquidated his assets, retaining only his share holdings as a silent associate. It left her incredibly rich and awfully jaded. She could never trust another man and at the tender age of twenty three she started to become the woman we see today. She had confided in Doug, that being a widow was the best thing that had ever happened to her and that she had never had a single day of regret about her charmed status.

"Wow, that is quite a story. No wonder she is so different." I was staggered.

"It explains some of it, not all. I knew she was going to screw you up. Like a lamb to the slaughter. I tried to warn you to be your own man, David. It's a lesson you need to learn fast if you intend to hang out with these people."

I gave a good deal of thought to Doug's advice. He was right, I couldn't just go through life being walked all over. I made some decisions over the next few days. I went back to work in the Foreign Office; I looked at Jason quite differently now I realised that he had set me up. I decided that If I was going to continue giving dance classes I would set my own rate, one that would be fair and professional, and that finally I would pay Maud back for her generous loan, no matter what it took.

A week later I went to the office of Bryan Hammond, Maud's solicitor, and signed my agreement for a private mortgage. The paperwork for the house would be sent to me as soon as it had been finalised with the Land Registry.

Then the next weekend I called my mother.

"Hi mum, how's it going?"

"Oh David, we sold the house, for the full asking price, isn't that wonderful? I'm just packing up our personal things now. I can leave all the furniture, the new owners want to keep it and have paid extra."

I was pleased to hear that she was happy and looking forward to a new life in the pub. She explained that she would cook the lunches while Harry would run the bar and handle the money. She would have a kitchen assistant and he would need a couple of barmaids. It was all very exciting and they couldn't wait to get going now that they had signed the lease with the brewery.

"You must come and visit, David. There is plenty of room in the accommodation upstairs."

"I will mum, I'll visit just as soon as I can. I'm glad to hear that everything is going well."

***

For the next few months my life seemed to have settled into a steady rhythm. I had another client now for my dance lessons and had also resumed my sessions with the Fortescue ladies. It was harder in their London apartment and very soon Camilla found the perfect solution. Her friend, a Lady Susan Heathcroft, had a very large 18th century house in Belgravia and, better still, a room that had originally been a small ballroom. It was a very elegant setting and the space was perfect. Lady Susan had a daughter, Sarah, who also wanted some lessons, especially after talking to Camilla who was now totally smitten with me. But I was learning, Doug's talk had got into my head and I was getting better at being assertive. I couldn't emulate Doug's masculine charm but I could keep my distance. And Doug was right, being aloof was working. I set the terms. I decided that we would meet three evenings a week to practice for which I would charge them a weekly fee, payable by cheque in advance. I also insisted that they wear the correct dress so that they could get used to handling the various costumes required.

When I finally got round to teaching the ladies to tango, the excitement of Latin American dance with all its sexual overtones had Camilla and Lady Susan gushing so much to their friends that I was soon getting more requests for lessons.

The extra money was going to pay my private mortgage to Maud.

I had been able to pay back quite a bit and felt pleased at my looming financial independence. All in all, the run up to Christmas of 1972 had seen a great improvement in my circumstances. If it hadn't been for my respect for and friendship with Doug I would have moved from the house share into my own apartment.

I hadn't seen Maud since the summer in Scotland but as Christmas approached invitations started to arrive. Maud was going to France but was planning a big party for New Year, she had especially invited Doug and I to accompany Jason. It would be a weekend of merriment and Jason was insistent that we all attend. Camilla had invited me to Scotland to stay with them for the whole holiday but I had politely declined. My mother's invitation to the Laughing Cow in Cobham had pre-empted any risk of me having to stay at close quarters to Camilla.

Lady Susan was keen for me to attend a soiree at her Belgravia House and had timed it for the weekend before the Christmas celebrations, especially so that I would be available. She was eager to show me off and had been hinting that she would be interested in investing in a proper space to teach ballroom. She assured me it was a skill that people of her class still valued and would pay for, and so a business opportunity that I should seriously consider. It would mean that finally I could give up my miserable job at the Foreign Office.

So the last thing I needed was to run into Clare while having a drink in Thistles Wine Bar with Doug. He was waiting for Sharon to finish her evening shift, he still saw her from time to time. Sharon must have told Clare that I would be in that night, I doubt she would have travelled all that way by chance.

"Hi Dave, how are you doing?"

"Clare, great. What about you?"

I couldn't miss the large bump, a red sparkly dress stretched across it making a statement. Look at me I'm pregnant. I felt slightly sick, I was sure that Doug hadn't been party to this set up. I finished my glass of wine and looked for an opportunity to politely leave but Clare touched my arm.

"Dave, I need a private word with you. Can we sit over there." She pointed to a table in the corner. There was no choice, I ordered us both a glass of house wine and followed her.

"You didn't ask how I was doing with the baby." She gave me a direct look. "You clearly don't care."

"Of course I care," I mumbled, guilty exactly as accused.

"Don't bother to lie. I'm not interested in what you think. I need some money."

"How much?"

"A couple of hundred will do, for now."

"Okay, I'll drop a cheque in tomorrow night, you can pick it up from Sharon when you see her."

"I want cash, I don't have a bank account."

"Okay, cash then."

"Make it three hundred, I need it to get some furniture for my new place. They've given me a flat in Bermondsey, it's a high rise but clean at least."

"That's good." All I wanted to do was get away as quickly as I could.

With the transaction done, Clare stood up and walked back to the bar.

"I'll be off then, I'll pop in tomorrow Shar. Dave will be leaving an envelope, to help me and little Joey out."
She blew Sharon a pretend kiss and left.

"Who's little Joey?" I enquired of Sharon when she got a moment to spare.

"It's what she calls the sprog."

"Sprog?"

"Christ, she's right. You are thick! Sprog, baby." She pulled a face and moved up the bar to serve another customer.

The next evening, I dutifully placed fifteen new twenty pound notes into an envelope and gave them to Sharon.

"Ta, I'll give it to Clare," she said taking the envelope and popping it in her bag behind the bar. "Just a tip, not for you, you're a prat, but because Doug will probably find out and tell you anyway. Clare is setting up home with Steve, a guy we both know from the estate. Be careful of her, she will squeeze you dry."

If I could have snatched the envelope back, I would have, but at least I knew the truth. Thank God that Doug had managed to keep Sharon sweet, otherwise I would never have known about Steve.

It was another lesson in life. I seemed to always be out of my depth, no matter who I was with.

CHAPTER 11

As the Christmas holiday approached I seemed to be increasingly busy with no free time to myself. The dancing lessons were insane. I was now travelling every evening straight from work to the Belgravia home of Lady Susan Heathcroft. It seemed to be turning into some kind of ladies social club, I regularly had five pupils to tutor but often as many as eight. All paid weekly with no fuss and my bank balance had never looked so healthy.

Lady Susan was way more astute than Camilla. She had looked after herself and her family after the death of her husband, she was in every way the matriarch of her little group. She could see a business opportunity and was lining up female investors. They were looking for the kind of premises that could be converted into a dance studio.
It was all totally out of my hands, discussed openly in front of me as though I was invisible, certainly not fit to have any control over any kind of business venture. I felt incredibly apprehensive about Maud finding out. I had ventured to suggest that I contact Maud for financial backing, but Susan was definitely not keen on having that woman anywhere near the project, which she had taken ownership of. She wasn't prepared to be side-lined by the overpowering Maud.

Jason and Doug had both noticed that I was no longer at home in the evenings, getting in late and going straight to bed. Within a few weeks Jason had wormed it out of me and reported to Maud.

"She wasn't happy, old chap. You'll get a frightful telling off when she sees you at New Year," Jason smirked.

It amused him to think that I had offended Maud and what kind of price I would have to pay. I felt slightly cushioned by my new clients who although not like Maud, still had considerable wealth and influence.

Doug was supportive, he couldn't personally see the attraction of ballroom dancing but had to admit that it was a nice little earner, and that's what counted in today's world. I hadn't discussed Sharon's revelations about Clare with Doug and he'd not broached the subject. Maybe telling me had been enough, Sharon didn't need to share her friend's secrets with Doug after all.

The weekend before the Christmas break, I donned my black suit, bow tie and shiny patent leather dance shoes. I'd bought myself a white silk scarf and a long black cashmere overcoat from Austen Reed to complete the effect. Then I made my way to Belgravia.

The door was opened by Lady Susan's butler.

"Good evening sir, may I take your coat and scarf?"

"Thank you." I felt inordinately pleased with myself, I was important, at a ball in Belgravia with the rich and powerful.

Lady Susan came scooting up to me.

"David, darling. You look wonderful. Come with me, I have so many guests who can't wait to meet you. They are terribly jealous that we found you first." Again that patronising statement of ownership. But did I care? Not really, I was the centre of attention, the favoured protégée of a spoilt woman. I was lucky to have fallen on my feet, I could have been stuck in the Foreign Office forever. Now a door was opening and I was determined to walk through, my head held high, my practiced aloofness covering my crippling inadequacies.

I danced with all the ladies, young and old. I was universally admired and assured by all that the dance studio would be a resounding success. Susan dragged me from lady to lady making exaggerated introductions.

"This is David, isn't he superb? We are opening a dance studio, probably in Sloane Street, we want to stay local. You must come and tell all your friends. It will be such fun."

"Have you found premises Susan?"

"No darling, not yet. But these people here own half of the properties in this place, one of them will know something, you can be sure. Well of course the Duke of Westminster owns it all really, we just lease but my family have had this property for two hundred years, so we're not going anywhere. I invited the Duke but he was otherwise engaged. Such a lovely man."

I couldn't really fathom what it must be like to be so secure in your wealth and yourself. I had never lived a life of poverty but this was something quite different, literally a world apart and I could see that I had only been allowed to participate because they wanted something from me. Doug was right, they were not good people, they were rich people, quite a different thing. I was going to be exploited that was for sure.

Stephen Fortescue had clapped me on the back when I was taken to be introduced to a group of very elderly ladies, who he was standing talking to.

"Well done old chap, I hear you are about to go into business, it's the talk of the town. Keeping everyone's ladies amused. Watch yourself, the hyenas might just rip you apart." He laughed loudly.

"What did he say?" An elderly seated lady obviously hadn't heard the rude comment.

"Nothing dear," Susan intervened, "just being his rude self." She looked pointedly at Stephen and pulled me off to the next group.

I left at midnight, it was enough. I was learning to keep my distance even though it had been hard work to keep out of Camilla's clutches. She had done everything possible to get me alone and even though Susan was irritating in her possessiveness, at least she kept me safe from Camilla's unwanted advances.

When I got home Doug was watching a film, his feet up, a bottle of beer in his hand.

"How are them up there in rarefied air?" he joked.

"I got out quick, indulged in a taxi home, didn't want to get mugged for looking like a toff."

"Quite right, but you are almost a toff now, laddie. Not long before you start inventing a completely different start in life."

"No, I'm not one of them Doug, they all know it. They treat me like a pet dog."

"Woof, woof. Get me a beer while you're standing up." Doug held up his empty bottle.

"Now you are treating me like a dog!"

"No, you're standing up, I'm lying down and have already drunk enough to make standing a precarious business."
I laughed, there was nothing like a bit of Doug reality. Especially after the evening of illusion I had just played my part in.
I gave him the beer and went upstairs, took off my toff outfit and wrapped my dressing gown over my boxer shorts. Then I returned, got myself a beer and plonked down in the armchair.

"No more money to that lassie Clare, do you hear," he said pointing his beer bottle at me. "I've heard she's living with some guy in her new council flat, bragging that they have some prat to pay for their lifestyle."

"I know, not about the bragging but Sharon kind of warned me not to be a fool."

"Good, whether the brat's your kid or not, that is not the action of a decent girl."

"I'd say I had a lucky escape, but I could do with a bit of the other sometimes. I'm not a monk!"

"Keep that boy in your trousers around those new friends. Don't be tempted unless you want to blow your business deal."

"I'm trying, Camilla is the worst. She is hunting me relentlessly."

"Stay aloof, it's your only defence. Of course you could tell them that it's me you're really after. That will push them back."

"Come on Doug, nobody fancies a hairy Scotsman like you. Get real."

"You'd be surprised sonny. I have that Sean Connery appeal."

"Right."

There was a good sequence in the film and we stopped our conversation for a while.

"Hey Doug, do you want to come with me to the Laughing Cow in Cobham for Christmas?"

"What? Laughing Cow? Why would I want to do that?"

"Oh, I don't know, because I don't want to face my mum and Harry alone, because I'm a born coward and you are like Sean Connery, fearless." I tried to make light of it, but I had been dreading going to stay with my new 'stepfather' around. It would be the first time I'd seen them since the wedding.

Doug turned to look at me, he seemed to be thinking.

"You'd better get me another beer from the fridge, then I can blame this decision on being drunk."

I jumped up and got the beer.

"Does that mean you'll come?" I said handing him a cold beer.

"I will be forever in your debt," I added dramatically.

"That's already a given, what the fuck would you be like without me to fend for you?"

I wanted to hug him. I didn't dare, he might have hit me, and I knew that a jab from Doug would hurt.

The door slammed and Jason walked in, slumped down onto the sofa next to Doug and nicked my beer off the table.

"Hey, that was my beer."

"Get me a beer then David, go on, I bet you got Doug one."

"Okay, but leave mine alone, I don't want to share a beer with you, I don't know where your mouth has been!"

They all laughed while I got Jason a beer.

"What are you up to?" Jason had a nose for conspiracy.

"I have just agreed to go to the Laughing Cow for Christmas to keep our boy company," Doug threw in casually.

"Can I come?" Jason looked genuine.

"What, to the Laughing Cow for Christmas?" I couldn't believe he meant it.

"Yes, if Doug and you are going, can I come? I can't go home to my mum and dad, they're awful, and Maud is away skiing or some shit.
Can't I come with you guys?"

"Okay, I'll have to warn my mum. I haven't been there myself so I have no idea what to expect, you understand that Jason? It might not be up to your standards."

"You can't both fuck off and leave me here alone, what about the three musketeers?" So it was decided, we would all spend Christmas at the Laughing Cow in Cobham.

My mother was absolutely fine about it when I asked her if it was alright to bring a couple of friends with me. The more the merrier and of course there would be loads of distractions. They had a band in for Christmas Eve and the restaurant was fully booked for Christmas lunch. She had extra staff booked to help in the kitchen and the bar, but extra hands could well be useful.

Doug had just invested in a second hand VW Beetle, so we all piled into the little car and drove out through Croydon to the Surrey countryside. The Laughing Cow was right on the village green and easy to find. We parked up in the pub car park and went round to the main entrance.

Harry waved to us as we entered the pub, where a few regulars were propping up the bar.

"Hello boys, here chaps meet my stepson David and his mates, down from London for the holidays." He introduced us to a few slightly inebriated looking men and called through to the back for my mother.

"Harriet, David and his mates have arrived. Come on girl, get yourself out here. What can I get you boys to drink?"
We ordered beers and Doug offered to pay.

"No, no, come on. Family here for the holidays, the bar's on me.

I didn't buy David a present!" he laughed.

I was shocked when my mum appeared from the kitchen, she was a diminished woman to the one I had known all my life. I could see Doug check me, he had met her before at the wedding. Jason didn't know any different. She had aged, deep lines now furrowed her face and she had lost weight. She had always been a thin woman but now she was just skin and bones. Was it too much work? I couldn't imagine what had brought on these changes in just six months. She wore a flowery dress with an apron over it but I could see she barely filled it out.

Her hair was blonder and she wore red lipstick, the effect just emphasising the gaunt, pallid features. I felt terrible, maybe she was sick. As soon as I could get her alone I would ask her some questions.

She gave me a huge hug, and I could feel her sparrow like bones through the thin fabric. "Happy birthday David, I'm so glad you could make it."

"He didn't say it was his birthday, you kept that one quiet lad," Doug remarked and mum just gave him a sad smile.

"He's always been shy, doesn't like any fuss." She reached to my face and gave it the lightest touch.

Mum showed Doug and I the rooms she had prepared for us. Jason seemed to be happy parked at the bar, drinking whiskey with Harry. It was true the pub had plenty of accommodation but it all looked quite shabby, like it needed some serious investment to bring it up to scratch. I wanted to talk to mum privately but she said she had to get back to the kitchen. She was cooking cottage pie and she didn't want to ruin it.

I popped my bag on the single bed. It looked clean but thread bare.

A stand in the corner had a blotchy mirror and in front a bowl and jug; they looked like antiques, but I guessed they had always been there. The pub was Victorian, behind the old world charm of the saloon bar the facilities were antiquated. The money I paid for the house wouldn't have been enough to make the necessary improvements. I came out of my room at the same time as Doug was leaving his.

"Is it okay?" I asked tentatively.

"Sure, no problem," he could see the worry on my face. "Just stay cool, it will be alright, we'll find out what the problem is."

"Can you see the difference?"

"Yep, don't freak out son, we'll find out what's happening here."

It didn't take long, Harry stood at the bar until it closed at three o'clock, he steadily drank his way through a bottle of whiskey with Jason. As soon as the bar closed Harry disappeared upstairs to rest before the evening session started at six. My mother fed us the cottage pie, no one else was eating and the pub was empty. She fussed around and I tried to get her to sit down and eat with us but she wouldn't.

"I'm far too busy to eat now, don't worry David, I will eat later. We don't open the restaurant in the evenings anymore. It was just too much work for me. I'm not really a chef, just a home cook."

"I can help you." I tried to get her to stay but she pulled away.

"I'll be back in a minute to clear your table." She smiled a thin smile and left.

Jason was digging into his food oblivious to the anxiety I was giving off in Doug's direction.

When we had finished eating I showed Jason to his room upstairs, he was just along the hall, next door to Doug. Jason flopped onto his bed. "I'm going to take a nap," he announced. I closed the door and went back down to the restaurant area.

Doug had cleared our table and was in the kitchen talking to mum.

He had removed his jacket and was drying up glasses. The kitchen was big and like the rest of the pub behind the scene, it was in need of quite a bit of upgrade. My mum had her arms in a large sink filled with soapy water. She had done most of the clearing up but I was going to muck in anyway.

"Is there anything else we can do to help you Mrs Taylor?"

"Well we have a band coming in later, I have to set up the bar area."

"I thought you said that you had employed extra people to help you mum." I could see that she was left to do all the work.

"Oh yes, Harry organised them but the kitchen lady has let us down, so we only have the barmaids who come in at six."

"Right then, let's see what we have to do. You direct us Mrs T and we will get it done in no time, then you can take a wee break before the night shift."

"Thank you Doug, but really you boys are on holiday, you don't need to help."

"Don't be daft." Doug gave her the full impact of his reassuring Celtic smile. "It's not a problem. Come on let's go."

I can't even begin to imagine what I would have done without Doug. I was so furious with Harry, he did nothing while my mother was being driven into the ground. We spent the next three hours setting up the bar, cleaning tables, shining glasses. Wiping down the back of the bar from the lunchtime slops that Harry hadn't bothered to clear up. The band arrived around five and started setting up their equipment, they spent about an hour then told us they would be back at eight to start their gig. Just after they left two barmaids walked in chatting. Mum introduced us and both women made eyes at Doug. They went to the back and removed their coats, they were both in their forties, puffed up hair and too much make up. Low cut tops revealing swelling breasts, I could tell that Harry had employed them, and probably not for their work ethic.

Doug and I stayed in the bar, the barmaids stood chatting. Around six one of them unlocked the main door and went back behind the bar. There was no sign of Harry but I could hear mum in the kitchen. She was busy preparing the food for the next day's Christmas lunch. It was half past six and I was sure she hadn't stopped since she got up. Goodness knows how early that had been.

Eventually, around seven Harry graced us with his presence. He looked a bit bleary eyed, he'd not long woken up but he had spruced himself up, wearing a red paisley cravat, and a rather flashy brocade smoking jacket. He said hello, waved across to us, and made a motion with his hand to ask if we wanted a drink. Doug gave him a thumbs up and went over to the bar. He got us two lagers and came back.

"I offered to pay again, but he wouldn't take my money. They'll go bankrupt at this rate."
I looked anxiously at Doug.
I noticed Harry had poured himself a large whiskey and a couple of gin and tonics for the bar staff. He was chatting to them both in an over familiar way, one of them reached up and straightened his cravat. I didn't like the look of that intimate gesture at all. At quarter to eight the band came back and started setting up and testing the sound. By then there were maybe six people in the pub. I noticed that there was nobody in the public bar, it seemed closed.

Then the band started their gig, it could have woken the dead and was way too loud and frankly too rock and roll for the clientele.
It was the end of any conversation and after a while Jason appeared.
He went straight to the bar and Harry put a large whiskey in his glass and topped up his own.
"This is great, a bit loud!" he shouted above the noise as he seated himself next to us.

I'd had enough after another half hour. I left the guys getting slowly drunk and went back to the kitchen to find my mum. She was peeling potatoes.
"Hey mum, why don't you join us for a drink, it's Christmas." I

tried to look jolly.

"Thank you David but I have all this to do for tomorrow." She pointed to the mountain of vegetables to prepare.

"Leave it, I'll get up early and help you, what time are the first tables booked?" I couldn't bear to see her like this. She was still wearing the same flower patterned dress, her make up was faded and her hair dank. I could see that she hadn't had any break to glam up and make an appearance as the publican's wife, more like the landlord's slave.

"No, I insist. Come and have a drink with us, I promise you I will help you get through all this lot tomorrow."
I had to take mum by the hand and almost drag her out of the kitchen. She seemed nervous, the look that Harry gave her was clear, he didn't want his wife out there in the front. I went up to the bar and ordered her a sweet sherry.

"It's Christmas, she needs a break."

"She doesn't like it out here, it's not her strong point socialising with the clientele. I'm the front of house guy."

"Clearly. Thanks." I took the sherry from his hand and went back to the table.
Mum sat on the edge of the seat and kept looking towards the bar where Harry was glaring at her.

"I better get back to the kitchen." she said after just ten minutes of looking extremely uncomfortable.

"No stay with us Mrs T," Doug piped up.

"I can't spend the whole night with these two." He indicated me and Jason and continued, "they're not the best company."
She hesitated and stole another look towards the bar. The place was filling up, Jason had spotted a couple of reasonable looking local girls and went over to stand nearby.

"So, how's the business going?" Doug enquired, although it was hard to talk over the noise.

"Yes, great," shouting over the racket.

The whole evening was painful, by ten o'clock the band packed up. It had been impossible to keep mum at the table, she had shifted nervously in the chair and at nine had made her excuses and gone back to the kitchen. The sudden quiet after the din was a welcome relief. The bar soon started to clear out and by the time the band and their mates had left we were down to maybe half a dozen regulars all congregated around Harry at the bar. Jason had disappeared with the girls. I hoped he didn't expect us to wait up for him.

The bar was still serving at eleven, although I couldn't see any money passing hands. Harry was looking worse for wear now, he groped both the barmaids as they made their excuses to leave, grabbing a large handful of one of their bottoms, before blowing a kiss to the other as they made their escape. I watched as he handed a twenty to each lady, which they both quickly pocketed. Doug had been observing the whole fiasco.

"I want to kill him."

"He's not worth the time in the nick, son. Lucky you took up Maud's offer."

"If she survives and isn't worked to death while he drinks away her inheritance." I was gutted.

"I'm going up, you should too. I suspect that Harry will be drinking well into the night with his cronies. No point in sitting here stewing, it won't help. We'll get up early and help your mum, I'm handy with the vegetables."

I nodded and we made our way through to the back. I was pleased to see the kitchen lights off so at least mum had finally stopped for the night, although I was sure she hadn't eaten.

I woke up early, I had a thumping headache. Stress.

I got washed, dressed, and went downstairs, it was only seven and still dark outside.

"Merry Christmas darling, I'm so happy you could make it." Mum was already up, wearing a plain red dress, the sleeves rolled up above her elbows. She looked pale and tired and had made no effort with her hair or make up.

I gave her a kiss on her cheek, "Happy Christmas to you mum."

She held onto me a fraction longer and I wondered if she was remembering happier times. When I stepped back she was wiping a tear away.

"Look at me, all sentimental in my old age."

"Are you alright mum?" I tried to look her in the eye, I wanted an honest response but she immediately started to move things around, avoiding any direct eye contact.

"Yes, fine, just fine. Don't you worry about me, you have to look after yourself now. As long as you are alright, that's all that matters. Maybe, I shouldn't have sold the house, it was selfish. What about your inheritance?"

"Don't worry, I'm doing okay." And I told her a little about my plans for the dance studio.

Just after eight Doug arrived and I felt relieved, it would take some of the tension out of the situation.

"Good morning Mrs T, you are looking lovely today. Happy Christmas to you madam and thank you for allowing me to join your family celebrations."

"Well, well." She smiled at him. "Such a charming Scots man. It's been a long time since I heard the auld tongue spoken, and so eloquently."

"Right, get me a knife and point me in the right direction. I will prepare the vegetables under your supervision Mrs T, if you will make me and the boy a coffee to keep us stoked."

We worked all morning, helping with the cooking and setting up the Christmas tables in the bar for the diners. It was a set menu. I looked at the table bookings in the large diary on the bar and hoped they were correct. Twenty four people booked between twelve and two. I moved things around, put out glasses and crackers next to each place setting. There was a choice between turkey and beef but no indication that there were any orders pre-chosen. The starter was only pate and the pudding traditional Christmas pudding and cream so we should be able to manage this. Everything was under control in the kitchen. Still no sign of Jason or Harry. I reckoned we were better off without either of them. Doug was helping mum so I filled the wine fridge with some white wine, then checked the bar, although I didn't really know what I was doing. But I made sure it was clean and finished washing up yesterday's left over glasses.

I opened the doors at eleven thirty to let some of the fresh winter air circulate and freshen up the place from last night's session. Still no sign of any barmaids or Harry.

"Nobody's turned up yet," I frowned as I re-entered the kitchen.

"Isn't Harry down?" Mum seemed concerned. "I'll go and check on him, people will be arriving soon."

She rushed off wiping her hands on a tea towel.

"Looks like it's all down to you and me laddie. She's a lovely woman your mum, I could have married her myself." Doug looked surprisingly at home in the kitchen and I imagined he had some previous experience. Everything was ready and the aroma was amazing. I was starving, there had been no time to stop since we started at seven.

"I'm pretty much set up outside but I've never run a bar before, I have no idea how to do things."

"You come in here and help mum, I'll take the bar."

"Hopefully Harry will arrive and help out, it's his pub after all." I couldn't hide the bitterness in my voice.

There was a terrible noise from upstairs, like something had been smashed. We both ran out of the kitchen to see what had happened.

Mum came running down the stairs, a tissue to her face. I could hear Harry shouting.

"I shouldn't have bothered him. I should have realised he was tired from last night, he works so hard!"

"Oh for God's sake, he does nothing and you look like you're nearly dead." I couldn't hold back any longer.

"No please David, don't say anything it will just make things worse."

"Leave it be son." Doug was pushing my mum back through into the kitchen behind his protective bulk. If Harry was coming down to face the music it would be him he bumped into first.

"We can handle this ourselves, leave Harry to sleep it off, no doubt he'll show his face at some point."
I felt useless, I couldn't protect my mum, all I could do was help her with the lunches and hope that Harry stayed away. Doug went outside to the bar. One of the barmaids had finally turned up.

"Where's Harry?"

"He's under the weather, we are all going to chip in and do the best we can, understood?"

"Okay, but he promised me double money for today, as long as you know that. I don't work on Christmas day for free."

"Don't worry about getting paid lass, just let's get the work done first."

Somehow we handled the whole lunch with only a couple of glitches. There was no sign of Harry or Jason but at least we put some money in the till. By four o'clock we had paid the barmaid and sent her home, she had worked for her extra money. Doug had made her wash up all the glasses and tidy up the bar before she got away.
Then we sat down together, opened a bottle of wine and had our own lunch, just mum, Doug and I and it was the first time that I saw some of her old self re-appear.

We toasted the chef and each other, congratulating ourselves on our success. Then we tidied up, still no sign of Harry or Jason and Doug and I got ready to leave. I didn't like to leave mum, but the place was closed for the night and Doug was keen to get back, I can't say I blamed him. We didn't bother with Jason, he was able to look after himself. If he got back and we were gone he'd just have to get the train home or go back to where he'd been.

On the drive home I voiced all my worst fears for my mum. I had known that Harry was a shit from our first meeting, now it had been conclusively confirmed.

CHAPTER 12

We didn't see Jason for two more days. He had certainly had an entertaining Christmas and declared that if he didn't get some sleep and rest he wouldn't last till New Year's Eve. But before he crawled away to his pit he made a disturbing remark.

"I thought that chap Harry was okay till I went back to get my things. He was totally drunk, shouting and pushing your mum around. I told him to lighten up, he just told me to fuck off, so I grabbed my things and got out of there quick. But I wasn't impressed old chap, not a nice sort at all."

I was sick, I had to get back there. I couldn't just ignore what Jason had said.

"You have to wait David, call her and see if she's okay, keep in regular touch, but it's her shout. You can't just drag her away if she's not ready to give up on her marriage."

Doug was right, of course, but what if something really bad happened? If Harry really physically hurt her? She had nobody, only me and I was pathetic. But I did phone, and with a lot of persuasion I managed to get mum on the phone.

"I can't talk now David, I'm working." She sounded nervous.

"Is he standing listening mum?" I asked, "Just answer yes or no, I understand, Jason told me."

"Oh, yes dear, that would be nice."

And then the phone was snatched away.

"Hello David, Harry here. Harriet just had to rush off, she's got food burning in the oven."

"I'll call back tomorrow Harry, I want to talk to her."

"Yes, of course, no problem, I'll tell her. Bye for now."

He put the phone down on me. I knew he was standing listening so that she couldn't tell me anything. I hoped that I had managed to make him think twice about his behaviour. I didn't know how this kind of controlling relationship worked, if the mental and emotional abuse would turn physical. But I was sure it would progress in that direction at some point.

I wanted to get her away, but she was his wife. Doug was right, it had to be her choice and she had to be strong enough to make that decision and keep to it. Was she ready?

I called the next day and Harry told me she was at the hairdressers. I doubted it. I told him I would call back and he was cocky as usual. "Yeh, sure, she'll be back later. You know what women are like at the hairdressers, takes ages to get all dolled up."

I waited till eight and called again, the hairdressers was definitely closed.

The phone was answered by the barmaid, I think her name was Joan.

"Hi, can I talk to Mrs Taylor, it's her son."

I could hear her mumble something, she must have put her hand over the phone. She came back with, "Sorry she went to bed with a headache."

"Can you tell her that I called and that I will call back tomorrow. Thank you." And I put the phone down, before she got to tell anymore lies.

I had to go there, I had no choice. Something was terribly wrong and I had to see her for myself. Doug had been following my trail all day and was waiting as I came back into the sitting room.

"Well?"

"Nothing, I still haven't been able to talk to her."

"I'll drive you down tomorrow." He looked at me seriously. He knew I wanted to rush there. I'd try one more call tomorrow but it was New Year's Eve and we were all meant to be going to Maud's party.

The following day I rang one more time, nobody picked up so

that was it. I made Doug a coffee and offered to drive myself, I could drive I had a licence. But he insisted and I was glad of his support.

We made good time and arrived about eleven in the morning. We went to the front door and hammered on it. Luckily Harry had been expecting a delivery and came quickly to open the door.

"Wait a second, I'm just getting the key," he shouted through the closed door.

As soon as it opened Doug barged in pushing him out of the way. "We've come to see the lad's mum. Seeing how she can't get to the phone, we thought we'd take a look for ourselves."

"Now, just wait a minute, you can't just barge in like this."

"I think you'll find that we just have. Go and look for your mum David, I'll keep an eye on Harry here."

"Look David, it's not what it seems." He tried to drag onto my arm as I went past.

"It had better bloody not be what it seems, you shit." And I shook his hand away and marched through to the kitchen.

"Where is she?" I was shouting now. "Tell me!"

Doug grabbed him by the collar and lifted him off his feet.

"Don't hit me, she's in the cellar."

"Cellar? What! You fucking bastard. I'm going to kill you. You better hope that she's okay!"

I ran to the cellar door behind the bar and opened the bolt. It was dark and it was difficult to see in the dim light. Mum was lying on the floor, I jumped down the stairs and rushed to her.

"Mum, mum can you hear me?"

"David is that you?" she responded weakly.

"Yes mum, don't worry we're here. We're going to take you away with us, you can't live like this anymore. Can you hear me mum?"

"David, I'm so sorry, please help me." It was a terrible feeble request and I felt awful.

I tried to help her up, I knew I wouldn't be able to climb the stairs with her in my arms so I pulled her to her feet.

"Come on mum, you have to be strong, one time for me now."
She clung onto me and tried to steady her shaking limbs.
We took a few steps and she buckled again. I held her up as
best I could with difficulty and tried to get behind her to push
her up towards the light. Then Doug appeared, he took mum's
outstretched arms and threw her up and over his shoulder. He
carried her up the steep stairs, she weighed so little. We walked
straight through the bar and stepped over Harry, who was lying
on the floor moaning.

"You can't just kidnap a man's wife!" he shouted after us.

"Shut up you fucking shit," Doug growled, "or she will be a
widow."
Doug carried mum round to his car and I opened the door and
pulled the seat forward. He pushed her in, none too gently,
and we put my jacket around her shaking shoulders, then we
climbed in the front. Doug started the engine and turned the
heating up high to get some warmth going quickly, it was
obvious mum was in shock. God knows how long she had been
in the cold cellar. Harry appeared round the corner, his face was
bloody where Doug had hit him. He had his fist raised at us,
shouting as we drove past. I turned to see if mum was all right
but she had collapsed onto the back seat.

"Should we take her to the hospital? Sorry Doug, I'm so upset
I'm no use at all. Thank you for hitting him." It was the first time
I noticed that Doug's knuckles were bleeding, it must have been
a hard punch.

"Let's just get her home and away from here. We'll take a good
look at her and decide what to do."

The drive was stressful, I kept turning round and covering
mum up with my jacket. She seemed a bit warmer with the
car heater at full blast but was still white as a sheet. When we
arrived outside the house, I ran quickly to unlock the door while
Doug lifted her carefully out of the back of the car and followed
me in.

Jason had heard us arrive and came from the front room where he'd been watching the unfolding scene from the window.

"What the fuck? What's happened to your mother David?"
We ignored him and Doug carried her up the stairs and into my room. I pulled back the sheets and we placed her gently in the bed, covering her up. It was the first time we had been able to assess the damage. She had a black eye, a purple bruise spread from the socket to cover the whole of her cheek. Her nose looked swollen and I was sure it was broken. I lifted her hand and she smiled at me.

"Jason, make mum a cup of tea and bring a glass of water."

"Okay." He looked genuinely shocked by her fragile, battered condition.
I rummaged in my bedside drawer and found some paracetamol pain killers. When Jason returned with the water and tea, Doug and I helped her up. She winced and I looked at Doug across her head.

"Where else does it hurt mum?" She was like a rag doll.

"My arm David, I hurt my arm when he pushed me down the stairs."

"Okay, stop." Doug put his strong arm around her waist and lifted her into a kind of sitting position.

"Thank you Doug, thank you all so much, I'm so ashamed," she cried, large tears falling down her ruined face.
Doug held her close to his big chest and gently rocked her, soothing her sobbing frame.

"There, there Harriet, don't you cry now. You're safe here with us, nobody is going to hurt you anymore. We will protect you."
And I could see tears on the big man's cheeks.

"We're going to have to take a look at you Harriet, we need to see if you need to go to the hospital. Here, try and sit back and take a sip of the tea that Jason made. Let's hope he has'ne poisoned you."
That produced the first smile of the day from all of us.

I put the pillows behind mum to help support her and she managed to smile at Doug, although smiling was painful for her bruised face.

"Maybe we should just take her to King's College Hospital anyway?" I questioned this home assessment of my mother's condition. But it was clear that Doug had more understanding than me of the level of shame and embarrassment these domestic situations caused to the victim.

"No, David. I can't go to the hospital like this, they will know."

"Yes mum, but what if he's done you some serious damage?"

"No, let me see if I can move."

She lifted the arm that hurt and let out a small sound.

"I don't think it's broken."

"No, not broken or you wouldn't be able to move it, believe me!" Doug replied. He gently moved the arm to check the level of mobility.

"Anywhere else, Harriet?"

"My face hurts."

"Yes, you have a shiner there."

"I feel much better now I'm getting warm." She was sipping Jason's tea holding the mug in her good hand.

"How long were you down there mum?"

"He went mad after you phoned, accused me of being disloyal to him. He dragged me out of the kitchen by my hair in front of all the staff and punched me in the face, then he opened the cellar door and pushed me in. I tried to stop myself falling down the stairs but it was dark and I just fell to the bottom and didn't have the strength to get up. I thought I would die down there. It was so cold."

She looked down at her dress and apron still in place, covered in the dirt from the cellar.

"I'm so sorry David. I'm sorry for everything."

I sat on the edge of the bed and drew her close to me.

"You knew he was a liar, didn't you?"

"Don't worry about that now. Everything will be okay, but you can't go back if he turns up all sorry and contrite. You know that don't you?"

"Yes, I know. It's over. It hasn't been a dream since I put the money from the house into his hands. It has been a long nightmare. I wanted to tell you at Christmas, but what could I say? It was all my fault. I've been stupid."

"I'm sure he's done this before mum."

"I need to get cleaned up, I can't lie in your clean bed in these filthy clothes."

"It doesn't matter, wait till you feel able. It's not important.

"I have nothing David, not even a pair of shoes."

"I know."

"Lucky your son's rich Harriet, we'll soon have you togged out, no need to worry about that."

"He's rich in his friendship with you boys," she said smiling at the three young men who had put her welfare before their own and had saved her from the brutality and degradation of her shameful marriage.

CHAPTER 13

None of us had managed to get to Maud's party in Oxfordshire. The next day at midday, the bell rang. There was a chauffeur driven Rolls Royce parked outside on the yellow line.

Maud stood on the doorstep impatiently ringing the doorbell. I ran from the kitchen where I had been preparing a small omelette for my mum to answer the door. Jason was still asleep and Doug was upstairs with my mum sitting on the end of her bed reading the newspaper out loud to her.

"David darling!" she said in a loud imperious voice ringing with irritation. "What on earth is all this? Jason phoned and told me the terrible story of your poor mother. Where is she?"
"She's upstairs with Doug, Maud, but she's very fragile."
I wasn't sure how my mum would handle Maud.
She pushed past me and walked straight up the stairs and without hesitation into my bedroom.
"My God!" she said immediately taking in the black swollen eye and ruined face. She opened her arms in a theatrical way and walked straight to my mother and very gently took the thin battered woman to her prodigious breast. And to my shock both women started to cry. They recognised the survivor in each other, something it would have been impossible to have known from pure observation.
"The bastard, the horrible nasty fucking bastard. David knew he was no good. Didn't you darling?"
Doug and I said nothing, we were both quite taken aback by Maud's actions and her genuine distress.
"What's your name sweetheart?" she said gently still holding

the sobbing Harriet.

"Harriet."

"Well Harriet, these boys will all be rewarded for their bravery and kindness and you will be safe, I promise you that. And I keep my promises."

She turned to me and Doug standing like statues in the room.

"If you approve, I will take Harriet with me. She will get the medical attention she needs and I understand far more about this kind of trauma than you can imagine. There are obvious needs to be taken care of. Your mother is a woman and cannot spend the next few weeks being cared for by you boys, for all you have done a sterling job so far. Now, I will help her to recover safely, it will be my pleasure."

She smiled at mum and mum smiled weakly back. There was a lot of emotional baggage to be dealt with and of course I was clearly not the right person to hear all the details.

"And we will make sure legally that your husband has no further rights over you."

Just like that Maud had re-entered my life and taken it over again.

I can't say I wasn't relieved. Doug carried the fragile woman down the stairs and placed her gently into the great limousine. The chauffeur quickly came round and placed a soft plaid blanket across her.

"Don't worry David," Maud said at the door, placing a gentle hand on my cheek. "It's for the best, I can help her recover. I know exactly how she feels. You can phone often to talk to her, it will be helpful for her to know you love her and care, and when she is ready she will be able to return to her life and her home." It all sounded so simple and it made my life so easy. But what kind of price would I have to pay for this exceptional kindness?

It didn't take long to find out. Throughout January I made the journey to Oxfordshire every weekend. I had been summonsed but also I wanted to be part of my mum's recovery. I had thought that the new year would bring me a new business and maybe the end of my purgatory at the Foreign Office. That wasn't the way things worked out.

On the first Friday in January, mum called me. She had been at Maud's for a week and asked me if I would visit. Of course I said yes, I wanted to see how she was doing so I took the train from Paddington with my overnight bag. Maud's chauffeur picked me up from the station and ferried me to the house.

As soon as James let me in my mother came running from the drawing room and straight into my arms. I dropped my bag and gave her a huge hug, pleased that she seemed so happy to see me and that she was looking so much improved, in fact like a completely new woman.

"Mum, you look so much better."

"Yes, it's Maud. She has been so kind David. I can't begin to tell you. Come in the drawing room and have a drink and relax. You've been at work all day and now had to travel all this way just to see me."

"I wanted to come mum, the last time I saw you it was a nightmare."

"Yes, I know. But I'm never going back to that nightmare David. Maud has shown me that I can have my own life back. I get stronger every day."

"That's wonderful mum, I'm very pleased for you."

At that moment Maud chose to make her entrance.

"Hello David, look how wonderful Harriet looks." She smiled indulgently at Harriet and no matter how much apprehension I felt, it was true. My mother did look like a new woman. I felt a strange unease.

"Yes, thank you Maud. I'm overwhelmed at the difference." It was my turn to smile at my mother.

"A woman's understanding David, it's what was needed. And I am privileged to be able to help. Harriet is a sweetheart, like you."

"James, champagne for our guests."

We were given a flute of Veuve Cliquot in the most beautiful Edinburgh crystal and we all clinked our glasses together, while Maud enjoyed her own largess.

"To the new Harriet." And we all echoed the sentiment with genuine enthusiasm.

Dinner was exceptional. After the champagne and a bottle of Nuit Saint George, plus vintage port with coffee in the drawing room I was flagging, but warm and happy, smiling as mum and Maud chatted on about the latest fashions.

I had just climbed into bed when I heard a tap on my door.

"Madam has asked can you join her in her room sir?"

Of course Maud was not expecting me to say no, how could I? I felt the stirring of anticipation at the thought of what would happen. I hadn't had sex since my visit to Scotland and I was after all a young man.

The room was darkened, only the smell of cannabis and some very low Moroccan fancy lights at the edges of the cushions where Maud lay, in a transparent silk kaftan. She looked exotic and alluring. I closed the door quietly and walked towards her.

"What are those things you're wearing David?" I hadn't considered my Marks and Spencer's pyjamas in my keenness to get to Maud.

I looked down and she burst out laughing.

"It's why I can't give you up David, you are so funny."

I wasn't sure that is what I wanted to hear just at that moment, it certainly deflated more than my ego.

"Come here and sit with me."

I went and sat rigidly next to her; she always made me feel somehow exulted and at the same time less than a man.

"Here smoke this and relax. Thank God for cannabis, it makes you see the funny side of everything."

I took a couple of long drags on the spliff and felt the instant release of my tension. I suppose the pyjamas were not exactly sexy.

"They're not exactly appealing, are they?"

"Why don't you just take them off, you are so much better without them." She laughed again.

I did as I was told, of course, and stood naked and vulnerable in front of her.

"That's better. It's been a long time since you and I have entwined our bodies, I've missed you. And contrary to what you might think, you have been the only one for some time."

She raised an arm to me and the silk slid down revealing a naked breast. She was so beautiful to me. She lay back and drew me to her, opening herself so that I could be enveloped in her arms and legs while entering her body. I wanted to pleasure her so much, I wanted her to look at me as a man, not a skinny boy. I pushed hard, trying to reach her inner soul. Lost in her woman's softness, lost in my total enchantment. I had dreamed of her, I had tried to take her out of my daily thoughts but in every way I had failed. I could not fail tonight. I kissed her body, every part of her precious form; words of completely dedicated love fell unchecked from my mouth in between kisses. I heard small sighs of pleasure and the occasional giggle as I said things so silly I would blush if they were ever repeated out loud. But I spent the whole night in adoration of this magnificent woman, who responded completely to my supplication. We slept together for the first time, I was not dismissed that night. I lay in her arms and she gently stroked my brow until I drifted into a deep sleep.

When I woke up, she had gone. But the cushions still felt warm and her perfume lingered. I luxuriated for a few minutes then found my pyjamas and returned to my room. I was tired but elated. I took a long shower and got dressed into casual Saturday clothes.

Breakfast was laid out in the dining room. My mother was sitting alone reading the newspaper. She looked up when I arrived and folded the paper away.

"David, Maud has gone riding. Help yourself to breakfast, I'm so happy you could come this weekend."

I served myself a large English breakfast and sat next to mum.

"Are you okay here?"

"Oh yes, I can't believe how much life can change in just one week."

I could still see the yellow discolour around her eye, a stark reminder of the previous weekend.

"Maud has been amazing David. She certainly has a soft spot for you, that's obvious."

"Jason, my housemate, is her nephew." I didn't want to give away my relationship with Maud, whatever it was.

"She has told me that it was you who bought our old house."

"I would have told you eventually. I just didn't want Harry to find out."

"I understand, he would have asked for money if he knew you had any."

"Mum, are you going to be all right here for a while? Honestly, you can go home whenever you want."

"Thank you David, I know you mean well. And I will go back to our house when I'm ready but Maud is doing so much more for me here. It would hard for me to talk to you about some of what has happened, I feel so ashamed. But Maud understands, she has had terrible experiences too and knows exactly what all this feels like. It really is helping me to be able to speak to somebody frankly about the whole sorry mess. Someone who is not judgmental and really knows what this suffering is like."

"Good morning you two. I'm glad to see you together. How are you feeling today, Harriet?" Maud came to my mother's side and kissed her on the cheek.

"Oh, so much better for having David here."

"Yes, I knew he was just what the doctor ordered." She smiled at me and winked.

"I'm starving, have just had the most exhilarating ride. We have to get you up to scratch David so that you can ride with me." She came across with the coffee pot and filled both my mum's and my cup.

"Do you ride Harriet?" Mum shook her head, "I'm happy to teach you while you're here."

"I'd love to learn. Although I'm a bit frightened, horses are so big."

"Just big dogs darling, nothing to be frightened of. David has had a go, haven't you David?"

"Yes, and I would be interested in improving."

"Excellent, I will arrange lessons while you are both here."

And that is how we spent the afternoon and the next morning.

I spent the next night in Maud's arms. I felt like I'd died and gone to heaven. I stayed an extra night and eventually arrived in the office on Monday morning, tired and slightly hung over.

CHAPTER 14

That night in East Dulwich Grove both Jason and Doug were keen to know how my mother was doing. I filled them in on her amazing recovery and how positive she was for the future. We had heard nothing from Harry. He would have no idea where she had gone and I had never given him this address, although he would probably find the telephone number written down somewhere.

I had cancelled my dance classes for that night, I had to get some real sleep. Although Susan had not been pleased, she kept her tone neutral.

"We'll see you tomorrow then David, if you are feeling better."

"Yes, of course. Just a slight cold, I should be fine for tomorrow."

She knew it was an excuse but I had to sleep.

The next evening I rushed straight to Lady Susan's for the classes.

Camilla was already there with Jennifer and Grace, so I started with Camilla, whisking her round the room to a waltz by Mozart. She was really improving and I found that I was enjoying the dance.

"I must speak to you privately David," she whispered as we twirled.

"I don't want Susan to hear."

I continued with the rest of the class, it was near to nine before I had finished and packed up my few things into my bag to leave. Camilla came past and slipped me a note, it was all very secret squirrel and I wondered what she was up to. Scrawled on the back was a message 'meet me at the Legends wine bar in the King's Road. It's very important, 10 minutes.'

I folded the note and said my goodbyes. I didn't really want to be alone with Camilla but I knew she had some gossip that must involve me, so I went and waited at the bar in Legends. She arrived ten minutes later, slightly out of breath as though she'd rushed. She kissed me on both cheeks like the French and sat on the high stool next to me. I ordered her a glass of Chablis and she started to tell me what this secret meeting was about.

"It's Maud, David."

"What is Maud, Camilla? I don't understand."

"Maud has spoken to Susan, she's furious with you," Camilla said knocking back her glass of Chablis and ordering another.

"I still don't understand. What has Maud told Susan to make her angry?"

"She's told her that you belong to her and that Susan can drop any ideas concerning a dance school or any other use we may all think you have."

"What? I can't believe that Maud would say such a thing."

"It's true David. She said she found you and that you are hers."

"Camilla, this is all ridiculous, I don't belong to anyone. I'm my own man."

"No David, Susan is going to pull out of the dance school and the classes will stop at the end of the week. Of course I'm happy to continue with my girls. We have so enjoyed the whole experience and you know how I feel about you David."

She looked down and I suddenly felt defeated. I took her hand and she gave me a small shy smile.

"I love you David, I will leave Stephen if you want me. I'm rich in my own right, you wouldn't need Maud's money."

"Camilla, I teach you and the girls how to dance, that's all. I don't want you to leave Stephen or anything else. I'm so sorry if you thought something more would come of it."

She snatched her hand away, hurt. Tears sprung from her eyes and I was terrified she would create a scene, I had seen her do it before in Scotland. I handed her a serviette.

"I should go, I'm sorry that this has all soured. I never meant to mislead anyone."

I got off the stool, picked up my bag and walked out into the rain and dark. The King's Road was still lively, cafés and restaurants buzzing with the young and trendy crowd. I went into the underground at Sloane Square and sat on a bench to wait for my train to Victoria. Well that was the end of my dreams. Was it ever going to be a reality when it depended on the goodwill of so many mercurial rich women?

Doug had warned me to be my own man, and I had tried, but when others hold all the financial cards, what can you do except try to please them? I just wasn't mercenary enough. Maybe I should be angry with Maud, maybe she had saved me from disaster further down the line.

Would I really have been able to control lady Susan? I doubted that I could. And I was never going to fall in love with Camilla. Even if I had lied to her for financial gain, she would have just played with me. I had to face the truth, I was a talented dancer, but that was not what these women wanted; it was just a byproduct, an excuse, useful. They wanted ownership and I couldn't understand why.

I was glad that it was dark and quiet when I got back. I didn't have to admit my defeat to Doug or Jason. They probably both had seen that this would happen. I made a resolution to keep away from women that night. But by the following weekend I was back in Oxfordshire in Maud's arms.

BOOK 2 - A NEW START 2012

CHAPTER 1

Florida was a strange choice for a holiday for me, but it was such a good deal. I was newly retired, at last, and unlimited by time restrictions. I wanted to go somewhere hot and it was only May, you couldn't guarantee the weather in Europe at that time of year. I had considered Thailand, but I didn't fancy being one of those lonely old men seeking young companionship in the exotic East.

I'd rented an apartment for a month, right on Pompano Beach, I couldn't wait to get away. I wanted to get up when I wanted, eat when and what I wanted and feel the warm sand under my feet.

Forty years in the Civil Service, starting in the Foreign Office and ending up in the Home Office, I was as regular and grey as anybody could hope for. I had a routine that I had adhered to, without flinching at the mind numbing existence it afforded me. I took the commuter train to London every morning at the same time, I returned in the evening in exactly the same way. Ate my microwave dinner on my lap, watched the news at nine and went to bed. It was always the same, I never deviated from my routine. The weekends were spent reading the newspapers from cover to cover. I walked to the local newsagents at eight o'clock both Saturday and Sunday mornings. Over the years I had lost the ability to sleep at random times and always woke at seven in the morning, every day.

Sometimes on Saturday evenings I went to the local pub and had a pint. It was still the same kind of old fashioned pub that old boys drank in, brown hues, with heavy leather seating.

Luckily it hadn't gone all up market catering to the young.

I don't know why I had ever thought life would be different for me. I had grown up like this and was obviously destined to be old, grey haired and single. I was no longer pencil thin but that was better, I had always hated my delicate looks. I had matured into a much better frame. You could say age suited me, now I could be counted as distinguished looking.

I had never married, I'd returned to Caterham after my mother's disastrous marriage to Harry Taylor and we had settled down into a domestic life together, just as it had been before. Mum had become an ardent campaigner for abused women and I had to admire her for the dedication she gave to that cause. Of course it had been Maud who'd set her up. They had established a charity, which bought safe houses across the Southeast for battered women from all social backgrounds. Mum ran the office and Maud put up the money to get things off the ground. But before mum died in 2000 she had established Government funding for their expanding organization and she was sorely missed, not only by me but the countless women and children who she had saved from lives of abuse.

Both the women I loved had gone in close succession. Mum managed to see the millennium before she passed away, Maud didn't make it and died in 1999. I was devastated and very alone. But of course I survived, as you do. I learnt to live a lonely existence. Occasionally I managed a quick holiday to Scotland to see Doug, he had remained my one friend over many years. He had met a lovely Scottish lass from Aberdeen on one of his trips home and had settled down close to where he grew up to get married and raise a family of three boys.

I never saw Jason after he married a French heiress and became a full-time jet setter. I occasionally saw them in the Sunday supplement looking very chic together.

As the holiday approached I felt myself getting excited, an

emotion that had been dormant for some time. I had bought myself, what I considered holiday clothes. I was so used to wearing a suit to work and cords and a jumper at the weekend. I had never been great with my style. It was easier, like most things to just establish a regular pattern.

I decided to go to Selfridges of all places and I'm glad I did. The young woman who helped me choose my look was really kind and helpful. She did great things for my depleted confidence and had me buying relaxed linens, pale blues which she told me matched my eye colour, and beige formal slacks and a navy jacket in case I went somewhere more formal. I felt quite rejuvenated as I got back on the train with all my carrier bags, containing the new me.

Eventually the day came, I checked all my documents at least twice before setting off. I had managed to get a direct flight from Gatwick which was great, it meant I could get to Pompano Beach which was about forty minutes north of Miami, it would help to start my holiday in the right way. No rushing, no panic, just calm relaxed travel.

Gatwick is a busy international hub and I arrived early, spent time wandering around the vast airport, bought myself a cream coloured Panama hat and had lunch before my flight was called. Luckily the journey was uneventful, and I arrived in Miami airport still feeling excited about the prospect of a month in a completely different environment.

I waited patiently in the long queue to get through customs then picked up my hire car from Hertz. It was all smoothly done, no glitches. I programmed the Sat Nav and set off for Fort Lauderdale which was in the direction of Pompano Beach. The tourist guides hadn't lied, it was a huge beach, holiday homes and blocks of apartments built facing the big blue expanse of sea to the Great Bahama Island.

I unpacked my things and hung up my new clothes. The

apartment was clean and modern, it had a large balcony facing out over the beach with a small table and two chairs for taking breakfast looking onto the view. The kitchen was small and functional, I didn't intend to eat in. I had done my homework and had my list of restaurants to try from Trip Advisor. I didn't bring my laptop, it seemed too work like. I had my iPad with a number of books downloaded onto it that I'd been meaning to read for some time but had never got round to.

It was early evening, I showered and changed into a pair of linen trousers and a loose shirt and set off to find the first restaurant on my list. The Calypso didn't disappoint, the shrimp was fabulous, the clientele older and relaxed. I had a Rum Punch cocktail at the bar and just soaked up the atmosphere. The beach stretched out just behind the restaurant and I couldn't resist a walk after my dinner to put my feet into the blue ocean. This is what I'd come for, peace as the sun set, the vivid colours that left a sea variegated from a bright green to a deep indigo in the distance.

When I returned to my apartment I was filled with a sense of achievement, even though I was lonely, but I was used to that. Tomorrow I would walk the beach and orientate myself, this was the start of my adventure and I couldn't wait.

My first two days were spent in total peace. I got up each day and made a coffee, which I drank on the balcony overlooking the beach. I had found a small store close to the apartment and had bought some very basic supplies.

If I walked a short distance there were chairs and umbrellas outside a small boutique hotel that I could hire by the day. I had bought factor fifty sunscreen for my white English winter skin but thought it best to be on the safe side under a sunshade. It gave me the added convenience of having a decent hotel bar and restaurant just behind me.

I re-started the Magus on my kindle. I had never finished

reading it all those years ago when Doug had given it to me to warn me of the perils of manipulative people. I should have, it might have saved me some years of heartbreak with Maud. She was everything to me and I was disposable to her. Capable of the most amazing acts of friendship and the most damaging rejections, I had spent years on her rollercoaster. By the time she had finished with me I was ruined, I had no confidence with women or myself. I had turned grey, all the colour drained from me. I knew that most men would think I was lucky to have had such an experience, but I was really in love with her and she couldn't love a man, her life experience had left her brittle and damaged. At best she cared for me and of course she was wonderful with my mother. They became firm friends, I was almost jealous as the years went by and Maud called and asked for Harriet. Not a word of interest in me or my non existent life. Like the shock of my father's will, I felt increasingly invisible and left out. Still, I didn't want to think about that now. It was a long time ago and I liked to think I was over it.

I had decided that I was starting to look less like a tourist and more like a local in my colour. I would risk a trip to Fort Lauderdale and take a look around. I took a water taxi to get my bearings in a city called the Venice of Florida. The onboard commentary was comprehensive and it gave me the layout so that afterwards I easily found the famous Hollywood Boardwalk and strolled along, selecting a place to have lunch and observe the people.

I booked my evening meal following the advice of my Trip Adviser list, so after showering and sprucing up I took the boat shuttle out to Hillsboro Inlet Park. There were great views of the historic lighthouse and I followed up as recommended by dinner at Cap's Place, the state's oldest restaurant. Originally a speakeasy from the 1920s, the menu varies depending on the catch of the day, but I was set on their famous crab cakes. I was glad I had booked because the place was packed, some kind of birthday celebrations going on, a huge table set up with a very noisy crowd of senior citizens, mostly women.

The wine was flowing, laughter and merriment all around. I felt myself smiling widely at their enthusiasm for life, after all age was just a number, my mother and Maud had shown me that. The crab cakes were the best ever, I had recklessly ordered myself a bottle of wine, I knew I wouldn't finish a whole bottle and if I did I would never get into the shuttle to get me back to Pompano Beach.

Swaying slightly I made my way to the toilets, on the way back I was grabbed by a very lively older woman who spun me around. I don't know why, but years of ballroom kicked into my drunken head and I took her in my arms and waltzed her back to her table. It caused an immediate uproar!

"Oh my God!" and "Look at that fella dance."

"Come and sit with us, don't let go of him Sadie, we need to capture him."

And just like that it all started again.

Sadie was giggling like a teenage girl, she hung onto my hand and I was made a space for at the big table. I tried to convince them that I was fine alone but they were having none of that, they were partying and they wanted me to party too.

I faced a barrage of questions, they absolutely adored my very British accent. Where was I from? Did I know the Queen? Had I been to Buckingham Palace? In fact I had, with my mother when she received an award for her work with abused women. We had gone to one of their famous garden parties and I described that to them, they were enthralled. They all lived in a community just south of Pompano Beach, mostly Jewish, mostly widows. There were a few men who had survived in their environment but they were still hungry for male company.

But the biggest question of all was where did I learn to dance? They hadn't heard of Frank and Peggy Spencer, that was a very British thing, but they did hold a tea dance at their community centre every week and they were totally adamant that I had to come.

Sadie pointed to Bill, who had to be at least ninety and said rather rudely.

"That's Bill, he's our best dancer, we need you David. Please come, please. I'll pay you."

"No, no, of course not. I'm here on holiday. I couldn't accept your money. I will come this Friday, I promise."

I stayed with them another half hour then went to the counter to pay my bill.

"The ladies have settled it sir." The young woman behind the counter was smiling at me. "You were quite a hit, British are you?"

"Yes, I am, but really I can pay my own bill."

"I'm sure you can honey, but if I were you I'd make my escape and just say thank you!" She smiled over as one of the ladies had stood and was singing Happy Birthday to the birthday girl, imitating the famous way Marylin Monroe had sung to John Kennedy all those years ago.

"I see what you mean. Well thank you, it's certainly been an interesting evening."

I couldn't stop smiling, what a night, certainly one for the memory bank.

The next few days, I took it easy. I was determined to take a trip to the famous Everglades and I contemplated the many tours on offer.

I spent lazy days on the beach and swam in the sea. I hadn't really thought about the invitation from Sadie and her friends to go to their tea dance, but when Friday morning arrived I decided a change of pace would be nice. I dressed in my slacks and blazer even though it was really too warm for such formal clothes, I had always liked to dance with a more structured attire. Call me old fashioned, or just old, it didn't matter anymore.

I took a taxi so as not to arrive too hot or get lost. The

community was lovely, large villas with waterfront lawns. A very grand gateway let you know that you had arrived in this wealthy enclave of senior citizens. The taxi driver had to stop and announce my arrival to the security at the impressive, ornate iron gate, then he swept me past immaculately kept grounds towards a pink and cream, very 1920's looking building with a long colonnaded porch. I paid and he drove off leaving me feeling like a fool. What on earth was I doing here, what if they had got the wrong day? I tentatively went to the heavy glass door and went in. Thankfully cool air conditioning hit me straight away, I was beginning to get very hot in my blazer.

I could hear music coming from behind another large ornate door. I pushed and popped my head around and there they were. Sitting on chairs around the hall, a couple of ladies dancing together, nothing in particular, just moving to the music. Then I spotted a few familiar faces and they spotted me.

"Oh Sadie, look. That British guy has come."

I walked towards their waving arms.

"Davis, thank you so much for coming to our tea dance." Sadie and her friends were smiling at me, nodding their heads.

"It's David."

"Yes of course, sorry David, we were all a bit tipsy the other night."

"But we are delighted you could come. We couldn't get over your beautiful speaking voice. So English."

As if I was made for this role and in my most British accent I asked,

"Can I get any of you ladies a drink?"

"You most certainly can." Sadie snapped her fingers and a young man came scooting over from the bar.

"What do you want honey? Scotch? My Archie always drunk Scotch, may he rest in peace."

"That would be perfect, thank you Sadie."

A small woman, with a beautiful complexion for such an elderly lady came and tapped me on the shoulder.

"I can dance."

"Wonderful, would you like to dance?"

"Yes, I can dance."

Sadie made a very rude hand signal, twirling her finger near to her temple, indicating that the little lady was not quite right in the head.

"What is your name, madam?"

"She probably can't remember her name, but it's Sarah," Sadie piped up on Sarah's behalf.

I stood and towered over her, she couldn't have been five feet tall.

"Well, let's dance Sarah."

I took her small arthritic hand in my left leading hand and stooped to hold her waist. Then we moved away from the table into the middle of the floor and I did the very best I could for this old and vulnerable woman. We managed to get round the floor a couple of times before it was clear that she was tired, and I returned her to her seat giving her a small bow of respect. She was flushed and looked very happy, a huge smile on her face.

I sat back down next to Sadie and her crowd. A woman, maybe in her early seventies leant across the table and touched my hand.

"That was very kind of you, Sarah is looking happy. They just ignore her, she has some kind of dementia. I'm June Wright by the way, very nice to meet you. I didn't go to the party the other night but I certainly heard all about you. You've caused quite a stir here."

"I'm not sure why June, I'm just a retired civil servant on holiday.

David McDonald by the way." And I held my hand out to her to shake. Without meaning to I noticed the most enormous diamond glittering on her finger. I'd never seen anything like it, not even Maud had owned such an object. She noticed, and I felt obliged to apologise.

"I'm sorry, I didn't mean to be rude, your ring dazzled me."

"It dazzled me too, when Mr Wright got on one knee and

proposed to me twenty-five years ago." She was smiling at me, apparently not offended at all.

"I'm sure, I would have married him myself," I joked, and she gave a genuine laugh.

"Do you dance June?"

"I certainly do David, I thought you'd never ask."

When June stood I could see she still had a good figure, tall and slim. This would be easier.

"Can we request music?"

"Yes, how shall we start? I may still have a waltz in me."

She went to the pianist in the corner and he started up a Viennese waltz. The whole room seemed expectant, what they knew and I didn't, was that June Wright had been a trained actress and professional dancer. But I knew in minutes, the elegant way she held her head, the lift of her arm to shoulder and the nimble footwork. June Wright could dance.

After a near on perfect performance, the whole hall were on their feet clapping. We gave a small bow and retook our seats.

"You've done that before I suspect?" I looked into very blue eyes.

"Once or twice." She smiled back.

"They all knew, didn't they?" I indicated to the ladies in the room.

"Yes, they were waiting to see how it worked out. I think they were pleased, don't you?"

"It's a long time since I danced with a woman who actually knew how to dance."

"That seems sad, didn't you keep up your dancing?"

"No, I looked after my mother until she died, well she looked after me. I always meant to join a club but just never got round to it."

"That's a shame, you have a real talent."

"Maybe, a long time ago." I felt introspective all of a sudden and went quiet.

After a few minutes of awkward silence, I was asked to dance again and escaped back onto the dancefloor with another elderly resident.

For the next hour, I was busy. When I finally got back to my seat on Sadie's table June was gone. I would have liked to have spoken to her some more. I sensed she had a story but I had always been a bit awkward with conversation, it was so much easier to express myself through dance.

CHAPTER 2

It was already week two of my holiday and I was excited about the trip I'd planned to the Everglades. I had paid a lot of money but I really wanted the experience of the hydrofoil. The high speed skimming over the water flats was really exhilarating. Alligators scooting away from us as we approached, wildlife of every description. The guide, a young guy in shorts and baseball cap with the company logo on his t-shirt was competent and knowledgeable and brought the whole watery world to life. We stopped at a wonderful waterside restaurant for lunch before heading back inland.

I was enjoying my leisure time, heading to the beach, lazing in the sun and reading under the brightly coloured sunshade. It was just what I'd been dreaming about over the winter months in the UK, as I'd planned the start of my retirement with this trip of a lifetime.

Since last Friday's tea dance I had made up my mind to start my dancing again, I'd really enjoyed dancing with the ladies and especially June. It had re-ignited my passion and even though I knew that I was past ever being fit or young enough to compete, I could still get a deep satisfaction from the pure pleasure that I derived from ballroom dancing.

The next Friday, I took a taxi back to Chestnut Grove and entered the community centre a little self-consciously. I hadn't been invited back and I hoped that I wasn't overstepping my welcome in this exclusive enclave.

I needn't have worried, Sadie rushed across the room and

grabbed my arm.

"David, gee! We thought you weren't coming and nobody was smart enough to find out where you were staying or how we could contact you."

She dragged me across the room to her table and I immediately had a crowd of ladies around me, all talking at the same time, all apparently glad that I'd had the initiative to return without them remembering to invite me back. I felt like a long lost son, everyone wanted to touch me. They had had cards printed just in case I returned, so that it would be fair and they would all take their turn to get a dance. It was quite overwhelming and very sweet of them.

The cards started to fill up and at some point I realised that I would have to factor in breaks for myself, I was sixty-two not twenty-two. I wouldn't be able to dance for three hours without stopping. Sadie went and spoke to the pianist so that he knew what dances to play and would be able to keep the music flowing. He had a drummer and a guitar player with him this time and I got the idea that some of the women were looking for more modern dances like the jive and tango. I just smiled, I couldn't imagine how this would all work out, it seemed to be a real medley, but they were so enthusiastic and had obviously been planning ahead.

I felt pleased when June arrived. I saw her slim figure enter from the garden entrance, she smiled and waved to me. She wore a floaty chiffon summer dress and held a straw hat in her hand, she looked like she had just stepped out of an English romance novel.
I finished my dance and took a break.

"Hello," I said going up to her.

"Hello you." She was really a very attractive woman and I hoped I was tanned enough not to go red.

"Can I buy you a drink? I get a ten minute break and that was only because I convinced them that I would die if I had to dance non-stop for three hours."

"Don't be bullied, David. These ladies are all used to getting their own way."

"I can see that."

"I'll have a white wine, Chablis I think."

"Right."

I went to the bar to buy June a drink but was again told that the bar was paid for. I didn't understand this and went back to June with two chilled glasses of Chablis.

"I can't seem to pay for anything around you people."

"Ahh, that will be Sadie, she is enormously rich and likes to pay for everyone, it's just her way. Don't worry about it, if you stay around you'll get used to it."

"Well I only have two more weeks, but being here has done me such a favour, I have decided to join a dance group when I get home. I was wondering what I would do in my retirement and now I know. I'll go back to ballroom, it's been great. I'm really enjoying myself, I haven't had so much fun in a long time."

"That's really great David, I'm glad us old girls have inspired you."

"I was going to say June......" But before I could continue I had been grabbed by Sybil.

"David it's my turn." And I was whisked away to a very slow waltz.

I was pleased to see that June was still there when I finished, and I rushed over and quickly continued, "I was going to ask you to dinner, maybe tomorrow?"

She just smiled at me, as I was dragged off again.

She made a motion as if for me to call her and I shook my head to indicate that I didn't know her number. I watched her walk to the bar in between my spins and saw her deliberately hand a piece of paper to the barman, then nod to me to make sure I'd seen. I gave her a thumbs up and she disappeared.

It was enormous fun, highlighted by a jive with Laura, a

seventy five year old woman who could move. Laura nodded to the band and a lively jive tune started up, she gave me a cheeky wink and held out her hand. Who would have guessed that petite woman could have moved so lightly and with perfect timing. At the end the ladies around the room were on their feet clapping madly and I knew I had to sit down for five minutes to recover.

By the time I got back to the apartment and dug out of my pocket June's mobile number, my confidence had diminished. What if she didn't find me interesting? Then why leave me her number? No, it was just me feeling nervous. All my life I had relied on two older women to guide me, this time it was me in the driving seat.
I eventually pulled myself together with a large scotch and dialled.
"Hello June, it's David."
"Hi David, I could see you were going to be busy." She had laughter in her voice.
"Yes, I'm a marked man." I felt myself wavering but summoned up my courage and blurted out after a small pause, "June, I wondered if we could meet away from Chestnut Grove?"
"Of course, much better. How about ice cream on the beach?"
"Okay, sounds perfect." I gave June my address and would meet her when she arrived at the entrance so we could stroll to the beach together.

The anticipation was terrible. I woke the next morning feeling sick, my hand shaking as I held my coffee cup. I changed my clothes twice before settling on a pair of light slacks and a pale blue linen shirt. I checked myself repeatedly in the mirror before going down to wait outside the building for June to arrive.
I paced the pavement left and right, squinting through my sunglasses for her taxi, wishing I had had the foresight to get prescription sunglasses. Finally, after ten anxious minutes the taxi drew up and June appeared, a vision in the summer

sunshine. Yellow cropped chinos and white linen shirt, her blond hair tied in a high ponytail and a white Ralph Lauren visor protecting her beautiful complexion.

"June!" Rushing to take her hand and help her alight from the taxi.

She smiled at the gentlemanly gesture.

"David, thank you." Taking my hand and feeling the warm touch. She stepped out of the taxi and for a second we were close. I went to the driver and paid her fare then returned to the sidewalk and in an act of enormous courage, I took hold of her hand again and smiled at her. She didn't pull away as she might have and beaming joyfully I led her towards the beach walkway.

"I'm so glad you came, I wanted to talk to you but not much chance at Chestnut Grove, I have a full schedule with the ladies."

"You certainly do, they love you, it's all they talk about. Sadie has plans to keep you here, you know that don't you?" June smiled back at him.

We found an ice-cream parlour with tables outside and settled ourselves facing the sparkling azure sea.

"It's beautiful, I love the sun and sea although you can see that I don't really tan anymore. Trying to protect what's left of my looks."

June threw away the remark while studying the menu of exotic flavours.

"If this is what is left of your looks I can't imagine how dazzling you were." I responded without really thinking.

"Wow, you are really a charmer David!"

"Sorry, I hope I'm not being too forward or offending you June. I didn't think, just spoke out my thoughts."

"Please don't apologise, I rarely have a handsome man compliment me these days." June looked relaxed and happy.

"Now, you are really embarrassing me."

"Why? Don't you think you are a handsome and, may I add, charming man?"

"No, definitely not. I'm an introverted old man who only feels confidence on the dancefloor."

June laughed. "How funny, it's so strange how we don't see ourselves as others do. They say you can't analyse yourself and in your case you obviously can't."

The server came and we ordered. The distraction gave me a chance to breathe in June's presence and recover from her observations.

"So, what is your story, David?" June continued as soon as we had placed the order and were left in privacy again.

I didn't really want to reveal my life's grey rituals and definitely wasn't ready to reveal my complex relationship with Maud. So I quickly fudged over living at home with my mother until her death, her wonderful charity work and my life as a civil servant. It didn't make interesting listening and it wasn't what I wanted so I quickly brought the conversation back to June. It was her story that I desired to hear, mine just bored me and I worried that it would bore her.

June listened, she could tell that I was leaving anything remotely personal out and couldn't believe that this was the sum of my life.

When I asked about her, she determined that she would not hide her truth.

So on that sunny afternoon in Florida, outside an ice-cream parlour on the boardwalk, David got to hear the story of June Wright.

CHAPTER 3

An all American life, from highschool to Hollywood. At nineteen June had left a Chicago suburb where she had lived with her parents and siblings and travelled to Hollywood to become a star, or at least that was the plan.

Her father, a manager at a car showroom, and her mother, a homemaker, had begged her not to go. She was their only daughter and they had indulged her. She had been taking singing and dancing lessons since childhood and was the darling of their small community, talented and beautiful, every high school boy had wanted to date June Kelly. June believed in the hype, she had been told she was special so many times that it was part of her psychology. She couldn't fail, she had never failed and her close knit family, especially her adoring father and brothers, stood in the way of anyone trying to get too close.

June was totally unprepared for Hollywood. She had nearly chickened out, her mother had cried so much the night before her departure. How different her life would have been if she had stayed at home, married a local lad and had a regular family.

Hollywood was a pit, waiting to open and swallow a beautiful but innocent young woman who believed in her talent. She shared an apartment with three other girls and worked in a local bar at night. Using up all her savings getting to auditions during the day and trying to keep up with the expenditure of clothes, make-up and hairdressers to keep her looking her best. It was relentless and destroyed her confidence as she faced constant rejection. But one thing her father and brothers had taught her was how to fight off suitors, especially the kind she met doing bar work.

She saw her flat mates fall victim to unscrupulous men, there were many tearful sessions with wine and pizza, while they all tried to console the latest victim. A married man who had no intention of leaving his wife, a guy with a string of girlfriends all believing they were his number one. Businessmen who knew somebody who would propel them to instant fame if they just pleased them first. It was a dirty business and most of the young, hungry prospectors didn't survive it and eventually evaporated home, if they were lucky.
Some never made it back.

June got lucky, a small part in a daytime soap paid her rent and she was able to give up her bar job and move into her own apartment.
Then out of the blue, after a year on set, she caught the eye of Steve Cole, the director.

Steve had noticed her before but had been happily married to his wife Marcie Grace, an actress with a couple of supporting roles under her belt. They had three children together. Steve was the faithful type, he loved his wife and children.

When Marcie's career took off and she was suddenly in demand, filming constantly, never home and worse, in love with her leading man, Steve's life fell apart. Marcie filed for divorce, moved into a mansion in Beverly Hills with her new lover and Steve's children.

Steve remained alone in the modest family home and noticed for the first time the elegant beauty of June Kelly.

June and Steve were married in 1974. It was a private affair on the beach in Mexico, hotel staff were their witnesses and although June had dreamed of a very different kind of traditional wedding with all her family in attendance, she had to admit that this was incredibly romantic and Steve was a perfect husband. Perfect in every way except one; after the birth of Marcie's third child Steve had had a vasectomy.

Life was good for June and Steve, they both had their careers and Steve eventually found himself directing bigger projects, he was moving up the ladder. They moved to a beach house in Santa Barbara and June auditioned and was eventually cast in more interesting film projects that expanded her previously limited soap image. She worked hard, taking daily lessons to keep her talents honed, and in the absence of children to distract her, she embarked upon a back breaking schedule of classes and work.

Finally a film that Steve directed made an Oscar nomination and for the first time June actually walked on the red carpet. It was a very glitzy evening and the film, although it didn't win Steve an Oscar, did get him and June an invite to one of the very prestigious after parties.
It was there that June met Henry Wright. Fate? Who knows what strange curve balls the universe throws at people and why.

June was forty, she had been happily married to Steve for twenty years, she had never regretted a single day. Her only sadness was that she had no children of her own and Steve's children with Marcie were determined to hate her. No matter how hard she tried she never managed to break through their icy disdain. Marcie played her part in it all. She hadn't lasted long with her new partner before it all went wrong and he dumped her. She and her children became victims to the Hollywood morality of constant marriage and divorce. Floating from one disastrous relationship to the next, the children dragged from house to house, school to school. Steve was distraught and had wanted to take them to live with him and June. It was understandable, but the children didn't want it, Marcie didn't want it and June didn't want it. The first serious cracks in Steve and June's marriage had started to appear.

Henry Wright on the other hand, was divorced, his children adults, his grandchildren settled in secure homes. He owned real estate, everywhere, LA, New York, Miami, London, Paris, Rome. His portfolio was endless, he was incredibly rich. The Oscar after party was held in one of his venues and by coincidence he was in LA so inevitably was invited. It wasn't his scene and he was leaving when a very beautiful woman pushed past him on the stairs and rushed out of the venue's large revolving front doors into the cold night. When he joined the sobbing woman on the pavement he could see that not only was she extremely distressed but also freezing having run out of the building without a coat. His limousine pulled up in front of them and without hesitation he took her arm and steered her towards the warm interior.

"You don't know me, but this guy driving does. I'm safe, which is more than you are, standing crying in the cold, on the edge of a street in downtown LA."

June slipped into the back seat without saying a word.

Henry handed her a white cotton handkerchief and she loudly blew her nose; he gave a little laugh but said nothing. When they arrived outside a very swishy apartment block he helped June out of the vehicle, still holding her arm, still without words, and led her to the elevator and up to the penthouse apartment. It was spectacular, picture windows looked out onto the nighttime vista of LA.

"I'm Henry Wright and you are?"

"June, June Cole. I'm Steve Cole's wife."

"Okay, Steve Cole's wife, would you like a brandy? You look like you need one."

"Thank you, yes. I'm so sorry Mr Wright to inconvenience you."

"You haven't inconvenienced me in any way," Henry said walking over to the bar and pouring two large brandies into heavy crystal glasses.

"May I ask you why you were crying on the sidewalk? Could

you have found the party as boring as I did by any chance?"
June smiled then, she couldn't help it. Henry clearly had a sese of humour.

"Here, come and sit down and tell me what happened to cause this tsunami of grief."

"My husband's ex-wife, his horrible children and his inability to understand. That's it in a nutshell."

"I see, complicated ground." Henry finished his brandy and refilled both their glasses.

"I reckon we needed more of these to get though this." He held out her refilled glass.

It was odd, Henry was a complete stranger and June was quite reserved normally, but she sat and poured out her life story, her deep disappointment at not being a mother, her unfulfilled life.

Henry just listened, he didn't offer any sage advice. When it seemed like June had confessed all her woes, he simply stood and called his chauffeur.

"Hi, Sam, can you bring the car round and take Mrs Cole home. Sorry it's Santa Barbara, I'll pay you overtime," he joked.

"Thank you Henry, what a hero. I mean it. I feel so much better now."

"Always a pleasure to help a damsel in distress. Here's my card June. If you end up leaving Steve, I have a vacancy." He smiled at her and she smiled back and for the first time she actually noticed that Henry was a very attractive older man.

Steve was beside himself with worry, he had no idea where June had run off to, she hadn't even taken her coat or evening bag. He'd asked questions but nobody had seen her leave. When he heard the limousine arrive in their drive he was shocked and angry.

For June, it was the beginning of the worst year of her life.

Steve wouldn't listen to any of her objections to giving his eldest daughter, Shona a home. Marcie had thrown her out when her drug problem had escalated. Steve genuinely believed that it was his fault for abandoning his children to Marcie's care and not fighting harder to keep them with him and June. Shona was a mess and desperately needed professional help which she completely rejected. She'd been in rehab before and had immediately returned to her habit the moment she was free. It became increasingly clear that all she needed from Steve was money. Marcie had refused any further financial bailouts and both Shona's brothers refused to have any contact with her so Steve was the only alternative.

Inevitably, June and Steve clashed regularly about their future with Shona in their lives. Everything had changed, the dynamics of their life completely altered by the need to babysit Steve's wayward daughter, always waiting for phone calls which invariably came in the middle of the night, Steve having to go and bail her out or pay for taxis to get her home to Santa Barbara. Finally, it became necessary to lock away any valuables, especially after June noticed pieces of her jewellery going missing. June tried to understand, but it wasn't her daughter and she felt like Shona and her problems were dominating her life.

The accusations were painful, Steve quite rightly understood that June just wanted Shona to leave, but he couldn't bring himself to throw her out. To where? The street? Drop her on the nearest park bench? It was inconceivable to him and unbearable to June.

June had kept the card that Henry Wright had given her. She had no intention of contacting him again and should have thrown it away, it had just sat in her dresser drawer for almost a whole year.
Then one evening, drinking wine, dejected and alone at home she decided to call him.
She looked at the card for some time, trying to summon up enough courage. Finally she dialled the number on the card.

"Hi, it's June, do you still have a vacancy?"

CHAPTER 4

June's narrative was fascinating, she was fascinating and I couldn't get enough of her. We had spent the whole afternoon together. After we finished in the ice cream parlour I took June's hand and we strolled along the boardwalk in the sunshine, found a seat that looked across the beach at the bathers and people tanning themselves on brightly coloured towels. It was an animated scene but I found it hard to look anywhere other than June, her life story had captivated me. I encouraged her to continue but as the sun started to set June decided it was time for her to leave.

"Can I see you tomorrow?" I asked hopefully. "Lunch? Dinner? Anything?"

She laughed, "I shouldn't monopolise you, David. You are on holiday, I'm sure you have many things planned other than hanging out with old ladies."

"I can't think of anything I'd rather do than spend time with you," I said earnestly. "That sounds so pathetic, doesn't it? I've always been useless with women!" I confessed, running my hand nervously through my hair.

"What a strange thing to say David. All the ladies love you, you must realise that?" She gently touched my cheek. "I'm busy during the day, and I believe the ladies at Chestnut Grove are expecting you for lunch, did you know that?"

I had no idea, presumably they had intended to tell me and forgotten. June agreed to dinner the next evening and I was ecstatic. We arranged to meet at her favourite restaurant in town at 7.00pm.

I made sure that she was safely in a taxi home then walked back to my apartment to mull over the day.

The very next day as I was taking coffee on my balcony I got a call from Sadie Levine.

"Hi David, me and the girls would love it if you could join us for lunch, we have a little proposition for you. Will you come?"

They wanted me to stay, and since meeting June, I wanted to stay. But how? I didn't have a visa to work and not enough income to live on the beach, this was a holiday, soon to be over. My mind explored all the possible scenarios on the taxi ride to Chestnut Grove.

I should have realised that Sadie was extremely resourceful, and usually got what she wanted. It seemed that I had always been the willing victim of rich women.

When I arrived, a staff member took me in a golf buggy, explaining that no cars were allowed past the reception building. We eventually pulled up in front of a very impressive residence on the pristine estate. It was by far the largest house on the site and Sadie was waiting at the door looking summery in a floral dress and straw hat.

"Come through David, we're on the patio. I got my kitchen staff to make us some lunch, just salad dishes in this heat."

Sadie introduced me to Karl Bernstein, her lawyer, his wife Cora and two ladies that I knew from the dances, Laura Cruz and Janet Warner. We introduced each other and complimented the fabulous garden and wonderful looking food. Niceties done Sadie got straight to the point.

"I own this place, not just this house, all of it, the whole estate," she stated matter of fact, waving her hand expansively like a duchess.

"I like you, you're an asset here, and if you want to stay as a permanent fixture, I reckon we could come to some sort of arrangement."

Karl explained that Sadie's husband, Arthur Levine, had built the estate and other developments in Florida twenty years ago, thinking that they would retire from New York together. He never made it, but Sadie loved the community and it became her home.

"We have been discussing some sort of contract David. Obviously, it's up to you, but if you're interested I feel sure that we can come to some suitable agreement." Karl's manner was very business-like.

"Yes, yes! Karl. I told him, just give him what he wants. I'm old, I can't be doing with all this cat and mouse talk!" Sadie took up the persuasion.

"You've brightened up our lives David. You see what it's like in this mausoleum, just us old birds waiting to die. The dancing reminds us of better days, days gone by when we were young and alive." She added, "I don't want to Foxtrot with Janet here, no insult Janet, but you know what I mean!"

"I can arrange accommodation on the estate, stay with us David" she wheedled in a plaintiff voice.

"Honestly Sadie, this is a truly wonderful offer but I have a house in the UK. I would need to close that down and there are restrictions to residing in the US."

"Not if you're rich honey. Karl here can sort all that stuff out for you."

I couldn't wait to discuss it all with June later that evening. I told Sadie that I would think it over and let her know the next day. Of course I would accept, the whole thing was like a wonderful dream that could actually come true. The holiday, the dancing and June.

We met at Fredrico's at eight o'clock. It was an Italian restaurant on the main street, busy but somehow intimate, low table lighting spreading a warm terracotta glow. An open terrace behind the main dining area was a green oasis with marble pillars and a central fountain, immediately transporting us to Rome on a warm summer's evening.

We were seated just inside but close enough to the terrace to appreciate the slightly cooler air that circulated nearby. The constant warm environment was one of the things I was loving most about Florida, so unlike England where only the brave remained in the pub garden once the sun had set and the chill set in.

I felt in high spirits and ordered a bottle of champagne to celebrate, ignoring the exorbitant price.

"To Florida!" We clinked our glasses and June smiled serenely.

"So, what did the ladies say to you this afternoon?" she enquired.

"They have offered me a job at Chestnut Grove, part-time, to teach ballroom dancing."

"And what did you say?"

"That I would have to think about it."

"Have you thought about it?"

"Yes."

"And?" June coaxed.

"It's a great retirement opportunity, to live in a community where I'm appreciated for what I love doing. The sun twelve months of the year, an income to boost my pension, and you." I dropped my eyes to the tablecloth, not wanting to see if June's face betrayed rejection.

She reached across and took my hand.

"David, I'm flattered. Look at me, please. I know how you feel, I'd be blind not to and I'm too old to pretend. But please don't make this decision based on me."

June was smiling warmly but I felt embarrassed and tried to cover it.

"Let's order, shall we?"

The food was amazing and the evening not a complete disaster. We ate, drank, and discussed the practical considerations that a move to the US would mean. There certainly was a lot to think about. June was easy and comfortable to be with and gradually I began to relax and not feel like I'd made a fool of myself. When we finished our coffee, she asked me to order her a cab and we parted best friends. I kissed her on both cheeks outside the restaurant as I held open the cab door.

"Goodnight David and thank you for a lovely evening. I do hope you decide to stay here with us." She smiled, then disappeared into the dark interior of the cab and sped away.

I was left confused, unsure as to where I stood. June seemed to like me, I was certain of that. Maybe she would come to love me? I was sure I was in love with her, it was all I could think about, she filled my mind. Images of her on the beach yesterday afternoon, holding her hand, the smell of perfume as she kissed me on the cheek. I was smitten, but clearly she didn't feel the same way about me.

I had a terrible night's sleep, going over in my mind the offer from Sadie and the rejection from June. What should I do? I needed somebody to talk it out with but had nobody. It was a decision I had to make alone, as usual. Finally, I phoned Sadie.

"Hi, Sadie. Can I come over this morning to discuss your offer?"

"Sure, honey. Just tell them at the gate I'm expecting you and they'll whisk you over. I'll get some coffee ready for you."
I arrived around ten thirty and was duly transported in a golf buggy to Sadie's front door.

"Come through, we can have coffee by the pool."
Sadie was sitting with a woman she introduced as her carer.

"This is Consuela, she looks after me." Sadie winked at her. "Isn't that right Consuela?"

"Yes madam, I try." She smiled warmly at Sadie.

"Can you get David and me a couple of coffees out here by the pool?"
Sadie walked through her large sunny sitting room and we made ourselves comfortable at a table with a large sunshade.

"It's beautiful here, don't you think?"
And it was. The lush, colourful garden with the azure pool, the constant Florida sunshine.

"Yet still you're not sure." She looked at me astutely.
I smiled weakly.

"So why the indecision? Is it all the bother of the move? I can pay somebody to help you with that."

"No, it's not that. It's a wonderful offer and I'm not turning it down."

"But?"

"I feel so foolish, but somehow I have to tell somebody."

"Great, and that any old person is me. Thanks!"

"No Sadie, it's not like that."

"Then for Christ's sake David spit it out. What's your problem?"

"I'm in love, at least I think I'm in love."

"Ahh, June." Sadie was so matter of fact about everything. "Well of course we could all see that and I'm sure June could too."

"How?" David was perplexed by women. All his life he could never really understand how they seemed to know everything about him while he knew nothing about them.

"Don't worry about that, If you don't know how transparent you are by now then just give up on it. I've got to say it's a most endearing quality that most men don't possess."

"So what are you going to do about it? she pressed.

"I don't know. I tried to broach it last night at dinner but June just shrugged it off and continued like we were just friends."

"Well David, that's maybe for the best. None of us are young here and some of us have had quite tough lives for all we have managed to come out well provided for. Give it time, love can blossom. It doesn't always hit you in the face!"
Wise advice that made me feel a whole lot better.

"So, I should take your offer and let time and charm win the day!"

"Exactly, well put." Sadie was smiling at me again clearly pleased with herself for getting what she wanted, as usual.

CHAPTER 5

It was strange to be saying goodbye to my home. I'd taken myself for a drink at the local pub on my last evening in Caterham. The barman, Roger, was keen to hear about my experiences in Florida and told me what a lucky bastard I was to be going back. I agreed but that didn't quell my nerves. It was an enormous step. Every day nearer to my departure date brought on another round of self doubt, and now all packed and ready to leave my life took on a dream like quality, every step forward done with resignation attached to a decision made long ago.

Sadie Levine was good to her word and everything had been accomplished without any tribulations. The accommodation, my contract, which was extremely generous, and my temporary visa all organised by the efficient Karl Bernstein, with little effort on my part.
Finally, the local Estate Agency had managed to find me a sensible family to rent my house on a one year contract. Apart from one crate approximately two metres square, shipped a week ago to the US, mine and my mother's lives were put into local storage and I was ready to leave on the adventure of a lifetime.

I didn't have the courage to keep in contact with June Wright personally but assumed that Sadie would be letting all the ladies know of my progress. I had not seen June alone since our dinner together although I had danced with her on the Friday before my departure from Florida. She had been warm and friendly but the intimacy that I desired was clearly absent. I tried to console myself with her friendship, it was as much as I could expect. But secretly I dreamed that on my return she would see that I genuinely cared for her, and that gradually she would melt into my loving embraces.

The taxi ride from Miami International Airport to Chestnut Grove was excruciating. This was Florida in the summer and it was hot, very hot. I could feel the sweat soaking my linen jacket, I was both excited and somewhat terrified, all at the same time. I had questioned my sanity more than once on the flight from Heathrow, what had possessed me to take these steps? After all I was a retired civil servant and really had only expected to lead a quiet, solitary life in my English suburban home.

When the taxi finally pulled up at the reception building, I was shocked to see some of the ladies waiting for me on the veranda, a long bunting strung across two pillars with the words, 'Welcome Home David,' in large gold lettering. They stood at my approach and waved furiously, huge smiles lighting up their faces, grey heads bobbing up and down in childlike excitement at my return. I was immediately surrounded and ushered into the large, airy reception area where a buffet and drinks table had been set up and a surprise party carefully planned for my much anticipated return. For all my exhaustion after the long flight and arduous journey to Chestnut Grove I was elated and emotionally overwhelmed by their welcome.

Sadie had been the instigator of all the excitement, I guess she rightly understood that this would be a big step for me. She knew that I was still infatuated with June, who was unable to make the reception, but had sent via Sadie her love and disappointment at missing my return.

"It's so good to get you back David, I was worried that you would get cold feet at the end." She took my arm and steered me to the table with bottles of champagne lined up.

"They couldn't wait to welcome you home. Watch your step, they are all a little tipsy already!" She winked at me.

Removing my jacket and sipping cold champagne was having an effect and I started to relax and actually felt happy to be 'home.' These ladies truly appreciated me, I wasn't alone, I was back doing what I had been born to do. I was going to dance all our sorrows away, and I couldn't wait to get started.

Young assistants, college students on their summer recess, took my baggage to my staff accommodation. It was a bright and spacious ensuite bedroom and lounge that incorporated a small kitchen, with large sliding doors leading out onto a long, sunny balcony facing the communal swimming pool. A distinct advantage, it was attached to the main building, making it possible for me to walk in and out without having to summons a buggy to get around. I thought that I might even buy myself a car and see some more of Florida. There was a large car park at the front of the building used more or less exclusively by the staff and visitors, few residents drove cars anymore.

My crate from England had arrived a few days earlier and I was able to take my time unpacking and reclaim my personal items. I pulled out photographs of my mother and Maud, one of them holding hands and smiling. It had made me slightly jealous at the time, hard for me to understand the close and intimate relationship that had developed between the two most important women in my life. There were a number of Doug and his growing family of rowdy boys and the most recent of the man himself, proudly holding up a small grandchild, a boy, of course. And there was Jason still looking cool and debonaire, smoking a cigarette on the terrace of a very swanky villa in Nice. How I missed them all.

Feeling far more settled and rested after a couple days of acclimatising to my new life, I wandered down to the large communal restaurant where the first dance class would take place.
The staff had already cleared the tables to the side of the room and the pianist, Johnny, was flicking through sheets of music

waiting for me to give him his brief.

Although it was early, the session was not due to start for half an hour, there were already a few ladies seated, gossiping and sipping cool drinks. They waved and smiled as I entered the room.

"Nice to see you back, man." Johnny held out his hand to shake.

"Wasn't sure you would make it, all the red tape you got to go through to get here. Anyway, the ladies will be pleased."

"We're going to take it easy today, Johnny, nothing too energetic! I'm still getting over the heat."

"No problem, man."

Two hours later, hot and exhausted standing at the bar with an ice cold beer, I caught my first glimpse of June Wright. A vision of elegance as she came through the room, stopping to kiss the cheek of a few of the ladies including Sadie but smiling in my direction. I was sure that she was coming my way. My heart was pounding in my chest like a schoolboy on his first date. Unconsciously, I opened my arms and she walked into my embrace, the feel of her warm body next to me and smell of sweet perfume on her neck. For her the return of a dear friend, for me the highlight of my world.

"David, I've missed you." She stepped back from me still holding my hand and studied me with a glowing smile.

"You look wonderful." It was all I could say. And she did.

"Thank you, I feel much better today for seeing you."

"Can you stay a while? Would you like a drink?" I couldn't bear the thought that she would be rushing off somewhere.

"Yes, thank you. Let's sit at a table and catch up."

I ordered two drinks and we moved to a table close by. I pulled the seat out for her to sit and she smiled at the gentlemanly gesture.

"I'm so glad you made it back. I knew that Sadie would get her own way," she gently mocked. "I'm sorry that I haven't been more communicative but I've been a bit under par."

"Are you okay now?" I felt immediately anxious that she was ill.

"Yes, I'm fine please don't worry, I'm sure everything will be okay."

She didn't elaborate and I felt unable to question her further.

We talked about England and the move and the cultural differences between the cousin countries. She didn't want to dance and I was quite relieved, it was hard, I had to remember that I was sixty not sixteen. Too soon she excused herself, she'd had a long day and needed to get home to relax. I understood. I had noticed a fragility about her and couldn't quite remember if it had been there when we had last met. Her cool blond looks seemed paler, but I wondered if maybe it was just the strong heat of the summer that made fair people pallid, a tan always makes you look so healthy.

I had so wanted to touch her hand as we had talked but felt nervous to initiate any intimate gestures in case she withdrew from me, and I sensed she would.

I waited around till most of the ladies had wandered away and then made my way to Sadie.

"So how did you like your first day?" she enquired.

"I think it went well, don't you?"

"I knew you were just what was needed to liven things up a bit around here." She smiled at me. "Retirement can be long and extremely boring, believe me. Even if you have money like me, you can run out of the energy to spend it." She laughed.

"Imagine saying such a thing! It's terrible isn't it. Especially when there are so many with nothing except poverty in this world."

"You could give to a worthy charity," I suggested.

"No, no way I can give my husband's hard earned money to those jerks! He died, worked himself to death, literally. I pay for all my family, that's what he would have wanted, everything.

They all have homes, cars, college degrees, all paid for by Archie's hard work. Charities pay stupid wages to unqualified people, take your money, give one cent to the poor and suffering that they supposedly represent and ninety nine cents to their overheads."

"Sorry I suggested it!" I said, trying to lighten the conversation. I had a number of charity subscriptions and felt it was the least I could do in the absence of any practical involvement.

Over the next few weeks we established a regular pattern of two classes per week and the Friday afternoon tea dance, that seemed reasonable. I had explained to Sadie that I was actually retired and had to have some time to myself to recover physically and hopefully to pursue other interests. I still wanted to be able to see more of Florida and occasionally get away to the beach for the day. It bothered me that I was the only competent male dancer, especially as the classes started to attract enquiries from outsiders.

Then one afternoon while waiting for my classes to start, June arrived and sat next to me at the bar. I hadn't seen too much of her and never alone so this was a nice surprise and it seemed clear that it was intentional. I seemed to have an unlimited tab at the bar, curtesy of Sadie. Luckily I wasn't a heavy drinker, else it could have all gone terribly wrong. I bought June a chilled glass of Chablis and we clinked our glasses together.

"It's lovely to see you. I'm sure you haven't come for a class."

"No, it was something that Sadie said to me in passing and I wanted to run it by you."

I was intrigued. Sadie knew that I was still holding a torch for June.

"I hear that you are getting some outside enquiries and was thinking that maybe you could do with some help?"

"Go on, I don't imagine that you are volunteering?"

"No, I would but I can't and it seems to me that the shortage is men, not women. But, I was thinking back to when I was struggling in Hollywood, taking classes I couldn't afford, working behind a bar at night to pay for everything. Maybe we should approach the Miami School for Performing Arts, see if we can get some young men here to help you with your classes, for payment of course. It even occurred to me that Sadie might want to set up a scholarship as an incentive, she can certainly afford it."

It was a brilliant idea, of course we would have to approach Sadie and I already knew her thoughts on charity. But this was a way of helping the community and maybe one or two exceptional students who didn't have the financial backing of a family. We decided we would approach her together, take her to lunch away from Chestnut Grove and try to persuade her that it would be a benefit to everyone, with very little actual involvement from her.

I left June to initiate the meeting which was arranged for the following Sunday. I felt quite excited by the whole adventure and more especially because it would be something that June and I would work on together. I saw an opportunity to spend more time with her and also do something valuable to the future of some struggling students. I appreciated that I had been so lucky all my life to have had the support and backing of firstly my mother, but later Maud and now Sadie.

I dressed carefully, a stranger looked back at myself in the mirror, no longer the grey man from Caterham, the habitual commuter in a gaberdine overcoat. I wore white linen trousers with a loose linen shirt in pale blue, the one the sales lady in Selfridges had told me matched my eyes and it did, blue, blue eyes in a tanned face, still a good head of hair, albeit a silvery white. I could almost be Italian. How funny that it had taken me to be over sixty before I actually thought I looked alright. It was extremely hot and I was glad that June had chosen a restaurant on the beachfront, hopefully we would get some sea breeze. The restaurant was crowded, but fortunately June had had the foresight to reserve and we had been allocated a table on the long outside veranda, looking out across the wide sandy beach to the sea.

Sadie ordered champagne and we all made our choices from the amazing seafood menu.

"Cheers! To us and to whatever you two have brought me here to discuss." June and I looked at each other and back to Sadie. You certainly couldn't put anything past her, she was as sharp as ever and had rightly surmised that we were up to something.

"David, you go first. What do you want? Money?"

"Not exactly," I managed to get out before June took over from my inept start and confidently told Sadie about our need for more male dancers, and how she had struggled so much as an aspiring dance student herself. With Sadie's approval and backing we could maybe establish some kind of bursary for one or more talented students. Hopefully in return we would get a good male dancer or two for our Chestnut Grove classes and Friday tea dances. And why not employ a few students as well?

It took a while and Sadie didn't say anything, just listened to June and I stating the obvious, that I was too old to take on more classes, even though there was clearly a demand for them, and that it would be an enormous boost for any student to receive financial aid to study their subject.

The food came and the tables cleared before Sadie asked the young server for the dessert menu, adding, "Hey honey, is this your only job?"

"No mam, I'm an art student. I do this at the weekends to pay for my living costs."

Sadie smiled at her and she went off to get the menus.

"Okay, I'll do it, but you two will have to sort it all out. I can't be doing with this kind of thing."

And that was it.

CHAPTER 6

For the rest of that summer June and I worked together. We were excited by the prospect of doing something really useful, not only for our little community but for the young dancers. We were both totally absorbed in our joint project and she was an absolute powerhouse of objectivity. It was far more work than I had anticipated and we found ourselves meeting up at least twice a week for morning coffee on my balcony, never at June's house. Any excuse to be near to her on my part, I would have seen her everyday if I'd had the chance. She was always warm and friendly but there remained a distance that I couldn't quite cross. I yearned to touch her and the slightest brush against her arm was enough to spark a feeling of deep embarrassment. I seemed to apologise a lot.

There were many meetings with the principal and tutors from the school, and we had to travel to Miami together a number of times. I discovered that June had a car, a Porsche Boxter, a beautiful silver beast that was parked up, unused. June hadn't driven for some time, not since she had been ill, she explained but didn't elaborate, so as usual I felt too restricted to enquire any further. I offered to be the chauffeur on our road trips to Miami. It was great to drive again. Like my mother, I had always felt exhilarated being behind the wheel and the Porsche was a delight. I had toyed with the idea of buying a car when I arrived in Florida, I wanted to see more of the place I now called home. June generously offered me use of her car whenever I wanted to get out. She explained that cars were not her thing and that she had been persuaded to buy the Porsche by a very pushy salesman, when all she had been looking for was a car whose roof came down, so that she could enjoy the open air and sunny environment, so welcome after living in a downtown New York apartment.

The first few meetings were just to convince the directors of the school that we were genuine. We offered financial help for students but in return needed dancers advanced enough to help with classes. On top of that we were looking mainly for males, and this was not a popular concept in society as it is today. Gradually, they began to understand. Florida's elderly population was predominantly female and the gap we were trying to fill was for the traditional male lead in ballroom, not ballet or contemporary dance. Sexual orientation was not a question, in fact it may be better to have less heterosexual assistance, as these ladies were susceptible and vulnerable to romancing rogues. Approaching things from this angle somehow made it easier to negotiate and in fact many of the students who applied for teaching roles fitted our script perfectly.

Sadie's lawyer, Karl Bernstein, drew up contracts for the students and the bursaries that were eventually accepted by the school. It was agreed that the award would be called the Levine Scholarship. Sadie had agreed to three to start, with the possibility of more if it all worked out.

June and I were thrilled with the progress, Sadie was amazingly generous. Each bursary paid not only the tuition fees but also a living stipend, it would make three talented students' lives so much better. Sadie had stipulated that the recipients had to be from backgrounds that would not be able to support them financially; she was determined that this would be for the genuinely disadvantaged.

Selecting students was June's responsibility. As she talked to the applicants, it had become clear to her that many existing bursaries went to the students who had been able to afford the very best tuition in the first place, their families wealthy enough to be able to pay for classes from early childhood, which gave them an enormous advantage. Both Sadie and June had come from ordinary families who had financial challenges and had not been able to spend unlimited amounts of money on their children. June especially knew what it was like to work hard and study with very limited resources.

When the first scholarship was awarded, we all celebrated.

"To Selena Gomez, our first student," I proposed and we raised our glasses, smiling at each other and enjoying the sense of achievement. It was a beautiful evening in early October, the sun was beginning to go down and cast a golden glow over Sadie's immaculate garden.

"And to you two, who made it all happen." Sadie leant forward from her white wicker pool chair and raised her glass us. I felt blessed, all my life I had been incredibly lucky to know the most marvellous, strong and resilient woman.

I may have never married and had the experience of children and a wife but I had managed by luck or fate to know women who had the courage to love.

CHAPTER 7

That glorious summer faded into autumn and finally winter, the long hot days gone and strong winds from the west sporadically whipping up a wild sea, and even the occasional outburst of rain. We all settled down at Chestnut Grove into our rhythm of dancing and the ever popular games nights.

I saw less of June, she rarely came to any of our planned entertainments. I felt that Sadie knew more about her increasing absence than she was letting on. A couple of times I had suggested that I would invite them both to dinner, ostensibly to discuss our students' progress but Sadie had always found reasons not to agree to that idea.

But by the time it was Christmas I was determined to stop being a coward and just visit June myself, unannounced. What was the worst that could happen? I spent hours in a local ladies wear shop choosing a hand painted silk scarf as a gift and decided that this would be my excuse.

Observing my reflection in the mirror, it was clear that I had made an effort and wished that I could appear more casual. I had showered and shaved carefully considering my shaking hand, inspecting my every move so as not to cause any damage. I combed through my silver hair and thanked my ancestors for not inflicting male baldness on me. Then carefully chose my military slacks and blazer thinking that at least I now could come under the heading of 'distinguished' looking. Maybe even a retired major or something like that.

I had ordered a buggy to take me to June's house. I felt

increasingly nervous during the journey and realised that she had never invited me to her home, maybe this visit was a huge mistake. But when we pulled up outside and I was deposited on the pavement there was no going back; she may have seen me and then I'd look like a complete fool.

I rang the doorbell holding the gift nervously in front of me, after a few minutes wait June opened the door. I knew immediately that I had completely messed up.

"David, please come in. I wasn't expecting any guests, you will have to excuse me. How I look, I mean."

"It's okay, I just came to give you this little gift for Christmas, I can go. Here." And I handed the wrapped gift to her on the doorstep.

"No, please come in. I owe you some explanations."

I followed June through the large hallway into a bright living room, with huge sliding doors leading out onto a large patio and pool area. I couldn't help but observe that she looked pale and very thin, but the sure give away was the headscarf that she had neatly tied round her head. It was cancer treatment, chemotherapy invariably made your hair fall out. I felt extremely uncomfortable, as though I had caught her out with some dirty secret, a secret that she had decided not to share with me.

"June, I'm so sorry, I shouldn't have turned up like this out of the blue. I feel awful, you clearly wanted to keep your condition private."

"I should have told you David, it's me who should be sorry."

We sat ourselves outside by the pool, but we were both awkward, self conscious for different reasons.

"I'll make us some tea, we can be English for a change. You probably miss some of the rituals of England."

Off she went back into the house and left me sitting looking out over her garden. I tried to work out how I hadn't realised. I had noticed that she had seemed to be more fragile, and that she no longer danced with me if she came to the Friday tea dance, she just sat with Sadie. But in my emotionally clueless male mind I thought that she was trying to avoid any repeat of my stupid outburst of devotion. All through the summer when we had spent time together it was always as friends, companions, even work colleagues; never intimate, always somehow guarded. It all made sense now, she had been ill the whole time.

June eventually returned with a tray and placed it before me on the table, two beautiful Royal Daulton cups and a matching teapot, sugar bowl and milk jug. I was immediately transported back to my parents dining room in Caterham, when I had first returned home from university, being treated like a guest with the best china.

"This is lovely." And I meant it. "It's brought back vivid memories of my parents. I don't think I have had real English tea since I arrived in the States."

"Henry always loved it. He adored England, we visited many times. I bought this little set in Harrods and lovingly carried it all the way back to New York in my hand baggage." She was smiling at the memory but looked pale and tired.

"You could have told me June." A bland statement really.

"I know, but I didn't want you to see me like this." She stopped abruptly and poured the tea.

"Anyway, now you know. I hope you understand."

"I'm in love with you June." I couldn't help it, the words just tumbled out without my permission.

"I know," was her soft reply. "But you see it's impossible to think of a future."

I dropped my head. Why June? Why now? What on earth had I done to make my life such a miserable mockery? I had to concentrate hard to pull myself back to the whole reality of the situation. This wasn't about me, I didn't even figure. The best I could be was strong and positive, hell, I wasn't good at that. Aloof was always my go to place; genuine strength, well that was for other people like Doug and Maud, and now June.

"How long have you been sick?" I didn't feel able to ask what kind of cancer she had.

"I was diagnosed with stage four breast cancer over a year ago. It's a miracle I'm still alive. I had chemotherapy and radiation treatment and I really hoped that it had worked." She stopped and her eyes filled with tears. "It hasn't David, it's spread."

You could have hit me on the head with a hammer and I'm sure that I wouldn't have felt it. I reached across and pulled her into my arms, she felt so fragile. I couldn't stop my tears. Why was my heart even beating? Surely it would stop.

We stayed together for some time, quietly weeping for all that could have been, for all that should have been.

"I want to look after you June, I don't want you to be alone."

"No David, you don't understand, I'm disfigured, ugly. I can't bear to see the horror in your eyes when you see what they have done to me. I just wanted to live, and now I know that it would take a miracle, more than a miracle."

"I don't care June, please don't reject me. I want to be with you, I only came back because of you."

She took my hand and gently led me through the house to her bedroom. It was late afternoon and weak sunlight came through the windows. She sat me down on the end of the bed and started to unbutton her shirt.

"You don't have to do this."

"I do, you need to see. I'm not a woman anymore. I used to be beautiful, really beautiful, but it's all gone."

She peeled off her shirt and I could see from the silk chemise that there was nothing where her breasts should have been. She bravely pulled the chemise over her head and revealed her decimated chest. Terrible scarring. She lifted her arms so that I could see that the marks went up under her armpits. Oh my God, how could you do this to such a beautiful creature? But I didn't feel horror, just deep sorrow. I gently pulled her towards me and held her closely, resting my cheek against the scarred tissue and she wrapped her arm around my head and held me to her. We stayed together in that loving embrace for a little while and then

I pulled her to the bed. Carefully, with respect for her fragile form, I undressed her completely, the sun still making patterns across the bed, and for the first time in my life I made love to a women that I loved and who loved me back.

When we stirred hours later the sun had gone and I carefully wrapped us up together in her bedding, always holding her close less the dream evaporated. She held on to me as closely as I held her and I knew she was frightened, I could feel it. I kissed her face and looked into her soul and made her a promise, that I would be there with her till the end, whenever that may be. That she need never doubt my love or commitment because she was the most precious person in my life and it was wonderful.

CHAPTER 8

It was raining, it was always raining in Caterham. I could have stayed in Florida, with the endless sunshine always there to lift your spirits and warm your face, but I didn't.

I had hung up all my pale linen trousers and shirts in the wardrobe under dustsheets. I couldn't imagine a time when I may need them again but I kept them all the same. A reminder of my dream holiday to Florida; a shirt unwashed because it still contained the remnants of the sweet perfume that June had worn.

I never regretted those last months with June, although I felt so angry with God for taking her away from me just when I had discovered real love, and myself, for the first time. The love I felt for June till the end gave me such a calm strength, but I couldn't have stayed on after the funeral. Sadie begged me not to go. She offered me more money, a house, her body. I laughed. She had known that June was terminally ill, she warned me that my heart would be broken, and of course I knew, but it didn't stop me from treading that sad road. Those last months were the best of my life because everything had to be said, everything had to be concentrated into such a short time. I held her hand till the very last minute, not bearing to turn away in case she slipped past me unnoticed to the other side. She promised she would wait for me and I promised I would find her even if it took an eternity. In the end that was all that was left.

I couldn't begin to imagine how my life would be now I had returned to my home, recovered my mum's furniture from storage and settled back into my routine, everyday ground hog day.

Then one morning something changed. My neighbours were a young family, ambitious thirty something husband, overworked mum, two youngish children and a small dog. It was a Tuesday morning, another nothing day, when I heard my doorbell ring. The mother stood there weeping.

"I'm so sorry to impose on you like this. You seem like such a nice man and you know, kind of lonely." An accurate description I suspected to an outsider.

"Well, we are leaving, you know that don't you?" I didn't.

"The problem is the dog!" She wailed some more. "I just love her you see. We can't take her with us to Australia and my sister who was going to have her has just let me down." More tears. I went to the kitchen and found her a tissue.

"Would you like to come in?" I suggested, I was conscious of a weeping young woman on my doorstep. I took her through to the kitchen, she was still crying.

"I'm so sorry. I know we have hardly spoken to you but I'm desperate!"

"I'll make us a cup of tea and you can tell me all about it." The English solution to everything.

Her name was Laura and after a few sips it all poured out, her husband had accepted a job offer in Sydney, it was a great opportunity for them as a family. But, they had a one year old French Bulldog called Moo who Laura adored, she was her best friend and confidante. The arrangement was that Moo was meant to be going to her sister's in London but at the last minute that had all fallen through. Now, with their imminent departure, Moo had to re-homed quickly and there seemed no solution other than the RSPCA. That sent Laura into another round of weeping. I could see she was heartbroken, a condition I could empathise with.

"I could take her, I mean, I'm retired. I'm sure the company would be good for me."

"Oh my God! Would you? Really?" She jumped to her feet and

threw her arms round my neck, crying more that ever.

"I can't tell you how happy I am that she will be going to a good home, but please if you can't manage, let me know. I'll give you all my contact details. I just want her to be happy and I'm absolutely sure she will make you totally happy!" She couldn't stop saying thank you. After she left my thoughts were, 'What on earth have I done?' I knew nothing about dogs having never owned one.

The next morning at nine o'clock the doorbell rang again. There stood Laura and looking down I saw a small black dog with a very squashed looking face, wearing a tartan jacket. She strangely reminded me instantly of Maud and I decided from there onwards I would in fact call her Maud, not Moo.

"I thought that you may want to start by taking her for a walk with me," suggested Laura. "Not far, she doesn't like to walk too far, little legs." By way of an explanation.

"Okay, good idea. I'll just get my jacket."
Maud was a delight, she walked to heel and never wandered off, even when we released her when we got to the park. Laura was right, after half an hour she made it clear that she was heading home.

"Well that went quite well, what do you think Laura? I think she likes me at least."

"Do you want to try on your own tomorrow?"

And that is how my love affair with little Maud started. When the day finally came for Laura and her family to leave I was actually looking forward to Maud coming to live with me full time. She was an imperious little thing, so unbelievably like her namesake it was shocking, and from the beginning she ruled the house and me with unashamed tyranny.

We established our routine and stuck to it; breakfast then our walk to the local park followed by reading the papers, then lunch. A little nap in the armchair in the afternoon, usually watching some antiques show, dinner and an early night with a book and Maud snuggled up next to me. I was actually feeling happy again, and it was true what Laura had told me about Maud, she was an excellent listener. Always pragmatic, we stuck to the really important things like dinner and treats. I quickly learnt all the foodstuff she liked, like sardines and beef liver and decided that only the very best would be good enough for my precious Maud.

The interesting thing about dog walking is that nearly everyone follows some kind of routine, so very soon I knew all the dogs' names on the nine o'clock schedule.

Weeks after Maud had taken up residence and my heart, we made friends with Sam, a Jack Russell cross. He was a bit cheeky at first but Maud soon put him in his place. He seemed difficult for his owner to control and rarely came back to her when she called.

One beautiful morning in July, before the park was flooded with school children for the long summer holidays, I was sitting on the bench overlooking the large green space and the children's playground. Sam came running from nowhere, wagging his little tail when he saw Maud, who was sitting like a good girl next to me, admiring the summer view. And a few minutes later Sam's "mum", clearly flustered and out of breath having chased him for some time, finally managing to grab his collar and attach his lead.

"Thank God, he finally stopped!" she managed breathlessly.

"I've seen you struggling with him before." I smiled up at her. "Why don't you sit down and take a minute to recover, you look like you need it."

She plopped herself down next to me and held out her hand.

"Geraldine Winter, nice to meet you. I already know you as Maud's "dad.""

"David McDonald, nice to meet you, Geraldine. Lovely day, isn't it?"

"Well now I've caught the little bugger, yes, not bad, better than all the rain we've had this year. I can feel myself shrinking!"

"Well, I'm off home, papers and lunch are calling. I will be preparing Maud's favourite sardine dish. Maybe see you tomorrow if the weather holds. Maud seems to like Sam and has a calming effect on him." And in fact Sam was sitting quietly next to Maud like a really well-behaved boy.

"See you soon David," Geraldine called as Maud and I walked towards the park gates. I turned and waved. She was nice.

Our routine started gradually to change. The weather held and so our trips to the park were regular and soon we were walking with Geraldine and Sam. Sam's behaviour improved and it seemed like he had eyes only for Maud.

"Fancy a coffee in the café, Geraldine?"

"Wow, that's a bit daring David. What about your routine?"

"Are you laughing at me? I'll have you know that I have been a bit of an adventurer in my prime, and also my not so prime to be exact."

"Now I am intrigued. You will have to spill the beans and tell me all."

It was all good humoured and I enjoyed her sassy company; she was a bit of an old hippy, wore flowing skirts and smoked the odd bit of cannabis. I admitted to smoking in the very far past, but certainly not for many years. I even told her a bit about Maud and especially the good works she and my mother had accomplished. Geraldine was impressed by that, but slightly shocked that I had remained a bachelor all these years.

"You're joking David, a good looking guy like you never caught. I can't believe it."

"Things never worked out for me, Geraldine, but I have Maud now and I'm not so sad anymore."

"That's sweet, I wish I could say the same for Sam, he's just like my last two husbands, wayward and difficult. Although poor Mr Winter went and died on me, not literally, you understand. A heart attack, out of the blue, just fifty nine. Terrible, I'll never forget that day, but I don't want to think of it now."

We sipped our cappuccino coffees and fell into an easy comradery, Geraldine and me. It was really the first time since June's death that I had begun to feel happy. But this time I pushed all thoughts of romance out of my head. I suppose I had always been at my best as a widow's friend.

ABOUT THE AUTHOR

Lizzie Diamond

Lizzie Diamond creates mystery romance novels with a twist.

The debut novel Dark Secret is set in Lassay-les-Châteaux, a picturesque town nestled in the heart of the French countryside, the perfect setting to combine a holiday adventure with love and romance, mystery and murder.

Lizzie has lived in both France and the UK. She is married and has three grown-up children and a very large dog.

BOOKS BY THIS AUTHOR

Dark Secret

In the tranquil beauty of rural France, Alex Taylor runs to her parents' holiday retreat to recover from the breakdown of her relationship. She needs time to herself to think and heal her broken heart.

Xavier de Verre, a successful French naturalist and reluctant television celebrity, has just bought his first home in the picturesque town of Lassay-les-Châteaux. Arriving for the summer, both are seeking an escape from their busy lives, unaware of the dark secret they would unwittingly stumble upon.

Nothing is what it seems, the peaceful façade is hiding complex relationships and a deep distrust of outsiders. A brutal murder changes the holiday setting into a hunting ground and very quickly things unravel. Waiting on his retirement, Inspector Giles Bonet is brought in to investigate because of the high-profile nature of the case.

Alex and Xavier are thrown together by fate as their idyllic escape turns into a nightmare. Can they keep the spark of attraction and possibility of a burgeoning relationship alive in the face of accusations, arrests and scandal?

This mystery romance with a dark secret and deadly twist shows the path of true love never does run smooth.

Secret Identity

Alex Taylor is madly in love with Xavier de Verre and living her fantasy life on the island of Martinique. She is embracing the Caribbean beach paradise and writing her first novel, whilst Xavier films his television show.

Yvette de Verre-Müller generously offers the use of her yacht for the wrap party but she has her own agenda. Certain Alex is not the right woman for her son, she enlists the help of Lady Victoria de Savory, who is only too happy to play along with Yvette's Machiavellian schemes and secure Xavier for herself.

Assistant producer Maisie Levine heads to the island for a few days holiday before her colleague Sharlene Cooper, daughter of famous movie star Grant Cooper, arrives to disturb her peace. Finding a friend in Alex, she helps her prepare to face the formidable Yvette.

Secret Disclosure

The last in the Secrets Series follows the fortunes of Xavier de Verre and Alexandra Taylor as their lives once again collide.

Both busy working on their careers, as the months went by they called each other less. Alex knew that they had no future together after what had happened in Martinique and she gradually grew distant, while her new relationship blossomed.
Xavier retreated to his work, where he was safe. Relationships were fraught with emotions he found hard to understand and he avoided meeting anyone new.
A chance meeting in London, and the flame reignited. Life forces always seemed to be driving them apart and the timing couldn't be worse.

Could their love, mature by experience, stand any chance of survival?